May 2016

5

To
Sandy

Enjoy
Idaho Author
Marilyn J Harris

Beyond the Idaho Mountains

- A Novel -

Marilynn J. Harris

Cottage Publishing

Cottage Publishing
Boise, Idaho

First published by Cottage Publishing 3/31/2011

ISBN-13: 978-1492294481 (CreateSpace)

ISBN-10: 1492294489

For information or to order more books please visit our website:
www.marilynnjharris.com

Or Contact:
Cottage Publishing
8530 Targee Street
Boise, ID 83709

Train up a child in the way he should go, and when he is old, he will not depart from it. PROVERBS 22:6

ONE

The flames shot up from every direction. I could not believe how quickly the fire had overpowered the magnificent mountainside. The beautiful forest that I once thought so breathtaking was abruptly bursting into multi-colors of crimson, yellow and bright orange. The helicopter climbed higher and higher trying to escape the vicious anger of the raging forest fire.

The fire leaped hundreds of feet above the trees as if it were reaching out and trying to grab the moving helicopter right out of the air as we flew over the burning forest. The helicopter bumped and bounced as the horrendous heat from the fire pushed then pulled on the structure of the flying vehicle.

The mountains looked so intimidating as I gazed down into the heavy clusters of trees that would soon be destroyed by the fire. There were miles and miles of inaccessible thick dark-green forest everywhere I looked. I was humbly overcome by the magnitude of the region. The rugged Idaho Mountains were so dense with trees; it looked like endless waves of black-green ocean gently rolling up and down over the steep mountain range.

My whole body trembled in fear when I realized the intensity of the past two years. As I stared down at the foreboding thick forest I was once again haunted by the thought of being imprisoned on the top of the mountain with no way to escape. Looking down at the forest from the air made my entrapment for the past 679 days even more overwhelming. As I watched from my seat in the helicopter I could easily see where the entire side of the mountain had slid away with the giant mudslide two years earlier. Most of the mountain was now steep, jagged rocks and dirt. As I studied the area from the aircraft I could tell that there was no escape in any direction. There was absolutely no way we could have ever gotten down from the mountain by ourselves.

The ominous lush forest rapidly burst into flames right before our eyes; followed by plumes of thick black smoke.

The helicopter again, bumped and bounced as it struggled to clear the trees. My little brother and I held on for dear life as we quietly watched the unchanging expressions of the two helicopter pilots.

Flying in a bouncing helicopter was a new experience for us, between the blustering wind and the angry forest fire raging at our feet, it was more frightening than either of us could possibly imagine. Suddenly we weren't feeling quite as safe as we had only a few minutes earlier when we were first rescued off of the mountain.

The pilots appeared to be having a difficult time keeping the small craft hovering high enough to keep us out of the trees. It seemed the strong winds and the extra weight of their two new passengers was just too much for the small helicopter to handle. I'm sure the pilots were then wishing they had never discovered us, trapped high up in the mountains, near the Idaho Wilderness Area. Because of their generosity we would probably all four crash into the steep mountainside and burst into flames.

The smoke was getting thicker and I soon began to cough. I started to feel light-headed as the smoke became so thick I could no longer see across the helicopter to where my brother had been sitting. I knew I would soon lose consciousness. I could not even tell which direction we were traveling, but I was sure we were going down. It felt like we were slowly falling closer and closer into the grips of the blazing forest.

I was certain that the pilots must have totally lost their vision too. The smoke was so thick I couldn't see the front of the cabin where the two pilots sat struggling to keep the helicopter on course. I wish I could let them know how sorry I was; for out of their kindness they too would soon lose their lives to the raging fire that was pulling the small helicopter down into the burning trees.

As I was drifting out of consciousness I could hear voices rambling through the air. I was having a difficult time understanding where the sounds were coming from. Slowly my thoughts began to clear and I soon recognized the voices of the two pilots. Apparently, I had underestimated the capabilities of our rescuers. The pilots were experts at what they did, because within seconds the smoke began to clear and my lungs began to fill with clean fresh, unpolluted air. I gagged and choked as I breathed in the wonderful scent of freedom. Then I realized that we had been going down, but the pilot was still in control. We weren't crashing to the ground, instead we were descending as we were preparing to land. We had made it down from the mountain.

As the smoke cleared I stared at the two pilots sitting in the front of the helicopter, their expressions still had not changed. They remained calm and confident as we continued on to our destination. They had flown the fire helicopter so many times before that they didn't need to visually see where they were going. The helicopter continued on for several minutes before we could actually see where the pilots were headed. They hovered around in a wide circle, before heading off to a clearing where the fire crew was busy setting up a large fire camp. I felt a little queasy as the helicopter made its quick descent and landed out in an expansive clearing.

The sky was still overcast from the sinister lightening storm that had hit the mountain only a few hours earlier, but to us it felt like a beautiful sunny day. We were alive! For the first time in almost two years my little brother Clayton and I were safe, free and alive! So, many times in the past two years we felt we would never see freedom again. Fighting off the overwhelming sadness and loneliness in our mountain prison had become our daily routine. I again inhaled the wonderful fresh sent of freedom and silently thanked the Lord for our independence from our imprisonment.

When the helicopter landed the four of us cautiously climbed out of the shaking vehicle, but the massive blades continued to whirl over our heads. Dallas and George, the two pilots pointed us in the direction of the fire captain then they turned around and just waved goodbye and hollered good luck to us. They climbed back into the helicopter to go refuel and head back to the fire. Within minutes they were gone.

They had brought us down from the mountain and saved our lives, then they just waved goodbye and shouted good luck. Our two heroes had no idea who we were or what we had lived through. All they had ever asked us was our first names. They didn't know where we had come from, or why we were even up there in the first place. The only thing that they had said to us, was that they were surprised to find us stranded that high up in the mountains. They couldn't see our beautiful family cabin from the air, because it was hidden in the trees. I'm sure they thought that we had run away from home because we looked so neglected and dirty. I wanted to tell them that we came from a wonderful well-to-do family. I wanted to say we once had lots of friends, and we went to an amazing private Christian school, and we lived in a huge house on a beautiful green acreage, with flowers, fruit trees and horses. I wanted to tell them how happy our family had once been; but it didn't matter anymore because everything was gone. So, I said nothing. They had discovered us trapped on the burning mountain earlier that morning then pulled us into the helicopter and never asked us any more questions. They silently flew us down to safety, and then went back to the fire. To them it was just all in a day's work.

My brother Clay and I stood in the middle of the massive clearing and stared as the helicopter flew out of sight. Then we did as we were told and we headed over towards the direction of the fire captain. People were scurrying in every direction; the fire crew was much too busy to pay any attention to us. The captain quickly ordered us a sandwich, chips and chocolate milk from the camp cook, and then he told us to go sit down under a large tree. He barely even looked up at us, he just instructed the camp cook to feed us and then he headed off in the direction of the main fire tent that was immediately being set up.

The large forest fire was only a few hours old and time was of the essence. We stayed back out of everyone's way. No one talked to us, or even acknowledged we were there. They were much to busy to be concerned about two filthy, orphan looking, run-away teenagers that had shown up out of nowhere. We overheard the men shouting to each other that the imposing forest fire had already burned several hundred acres because of the high winds. They said that it was raging out of control up near the Wilderness Area where they had found us.

We knew that there had been numerous lightning strikes in that whole area, because we were directly in the center of the storm up on our mountain. We could tell as we flew over the fire in the rescue helicopter that the fire crews would soon be dealing with a multitude of hot spots at one time.

We sat quietly under the huge shade tree just as we were told to do, and ate our food. Sitting peacefully under a tree for several hours was much easier for my little brother and I than it would be for most teenagers, because in the past two years being silent had become a normal way of life for us. We were both very content to sit and quietly eat, because the camp cook had given us real ham and real cheese on real bread with a carton of real milk. We were in heaven. I closed my eyes and savored the large carton of chocolate milk I had been given. Milk! Fresh ice-cold delicious chocolate milk. The camp cook noticed how much I was enjoying the chocolate milk, so he gave me two more cartons then he walked off mumbling something about me drowning myself in milk.

He then mumbled something else, but I was enjoying my fresh ice-cold milk too much to reply.

TWO

The fire captain gathered up his men and had them sit down out under the big tree right where we'd been sitting. He talked to his men as if we weren't even there. He said, "Because of the severe winds the fire has changed direction and is now veering off towards the small town of Riggins. We hope to keep it from crossing the river before it reaches the quiet little canyon town. The fire has already burned several small cabins and it will soon threaten more homes and many large structures if we can't get it re-directed. We will know within the next three hours if we need to evacuate the entire town." He told his men, "Our main concern is to keep it contained to the high mountain region until we can get it under control, but the area we are dealing with is so steep and jagged that it is very difficult to even get to, let alone contain it. My lead pilots, Dallas and George were the first to fly over the strike zone soon after the lightening had first hit. I sent them out immediately to scout out the rugged territory." He continued, "They have already dumped water on a few of the main hot spots, but they reported back that the rough mountain location is very difficult to get fires crews into. It is the Wilderness Area and there are no roads for the crews to travel on."

As the captain talked to his men I thought about the two helicopter pilots, Dallas and George. Luckily, for us they were sent to check out the fire, and they were sent directly to our area. As I sat there trying to listen to the captain speak I couldn't help but think, was it luck, or was it all in God's plan for my little brother and I? No one even knew that we were up there, but the pilots were sent straight to our mountain.

None of us knows for sure how a prayer will ever be answered. I thought back to the last letter my beloved mother had left for Clayton and I, up at our family cabin on Moon Mountain. It was written only a few weeks before she died last summer. She wrote, "My dying prayer is that you will each be protected and somehow live a full and wonderful life. Always remember God loves you. Your father and I cherished you more than life itself."

"Were the two pilots the answer to my dying mother's prayer?" I questioned. I guess I will never know for sure, all I know is that they were sent precisely to our mountain and they brought us down to safety just in time.

We felt a little intrusive as we silently sat back and listened to all of the commands of the fire captain. We really didn't belong there and we shouldn't be listening, but we really didn't belong anywhere and we were just sitting where we were instructed to sit.

As I listened to the fire captain talk, the seriousness of the devastating fire thoroughly sickened me. He was talking about the same mountain area where we had been trapped up in our family's cabin, for almost two years.

My brother and I had been left all alone after the tragic deaths of our prominent parents, Clinton William Richardson II and Marci Nicole Richardson. Our parents had both died up on the mountain, leaving my little brother and I all alone trying to survive in our isolated dream house.

My poor bewildered father had carelessly driven us up to Moon Mountain two years ago, after his giant corporation collapsed. People were angry with him because he was the CEO of the company, and they felt he hadn't managed the corporation correctly. The entire company went bankrupt and thousands of people had lost their jobs. People from the company were threatening him and calling our house and screaming accusations at our mother. My father feared for our safety, so he took us up to our remote family cabin where he knew we would be safe and have plenty of food, water and shelter. Up at the cabin, we would be protected from all of the public ridicule that was going on down in the valley. My mother told us that his plan was to keep us hidden away for a few days while all of the scandal and death-threats calmed down.

I felt queasy thinking about that dreadful morning twenty-three months ago. That foreboding morning would change my life forever. That was the day I lost my father and my freedom. I had loved my dad so much. He was my idol. I wanted to be just like him when I grew up. He was kind, gentle and intelligent, but when the overseas market destroyed his company it changed him completely. He became very withdrawn and severely depressed, and towards the end he had even stopped talking to any of us. All he could think about was getting our family to safety. His sole focus was to quietly hide us away, high up in the rugged Idaho Mountains where no one could find us.

We arrived at our secret hiding place up at our cabin on Moon Mountain late one Wednesday evening, almost two years ago. It was raining so hard that night that the rain was overflowing the rain gutters and raging down the mountainside like a wild uncontrolled river. Our family had never seen such violent rain. It was terrifying. I remember when we nervously went to bed that night it was very difficult trying to fall asleep. I had so many questions I wanted to ask my dad, but as I tossed and turned in my bed, I could hear him groaning in the other room as he tried to sleep. He was whimpering so loud that I could hear his moans above the outrage of the rain pounding on the cabin's metal roof.

Finally, sometime during the night I got tired enough to fall asleep. Then at daybreak, Thursday morning my father got up before anyone else was awake, and he climbed into the Hummer and secretly headed back down the mountain towards town. He knew none of us would ever allow him to leave the cabin alone, so he tried to sneak away before anyone was awake.

For as long as I live, I will never forget that horrible day. I woke up just in time to find him driving rapidly away from the cabin. I slipped and slid after him in my bare feet screaming for him not to leave, but it was still raining, and the noise of the rain drowned out my screams. It had rained so much the night before and the mud was so deep, that I was unable to compete with the massive tires of the Hummer, I couldn't catch him.

Then I watched in horror as my despondent father lost control of his vehicle and fishtailed back and forth in the slippery mud before propelling through the air and rolling down the steep embankment. The violence of the rolling vehicle caused the mountain to give way and the entire mountain became one giant mudslide. It looked like miles of the mountain were gone. Trees, shrubs and gigantic boulders joined in the turbulence as they too raced to the bottom of the deep ravine. When the Hummer stopped rolling and came to rest at the bottom of the canyon, the mud, trees and boulders from the mountain completely buried my father. The whole side of the mountain had given way and the old road that we had traveled up on was gone. Moon Mountain had become my father's grave. Leaving my mother, brother and I trapped on top of the mountain with no way to get home.

My whole body still quivers as I sit and dwell on the memory of that horrendous morning two years ago. I was only fourteen years old and in the ninth grade at a private Christian school. My world was perfect. I had a large group of friends, a beautiful home, my family, and I even had my very first car, but that morning two years ago changed my life forever.

My little brother's name is Clayton, and my name is Will. My full name is Clinton William Richardson, just like my father, but I am the III. My father Clint was named after his father, and I was named after him. It was an honor to be the third generation with my grandfather's name.

As I sat there listening to the fire captain talking to his men, I again thought about my father. I knew my father had been dead for a long time, yet it seemed like only yesterday. I still missed him so much. The only family I have left in the world is my little brother. We have a Grandma and Grandpa Richardson that live in Florida, but we haven't seen them for over two years. They don't even know what happened to us. That rainy October evening, our whole family just vanished.

My parents had never taken anyone up to our remote property with us, so no one knew exactly where it was located. It was high up on a rugged mountain, bordering near The Idaho Wilderness Area. You would not find Moon Mountain written on any Idaho map, because that was our family's private name for our secret mountain hideaway.

My father had personally created our beautiful secluded paradise several years ago as a special anniversary gift for my mother. The terrain was very steep, so my dad had all of the builders and building materials flown in by helicopter. He had also flown in many years supply of food and cut-up firewood for the cook stove. When I was young our family adored our beautiful cabin on Moon Mountain. It was my parent's pride and joy.

After losing both of our parents and being trapped on the mountain for so long, it no longer held the fond memories for my brother and I that it once did. It had ultimately become our prison.

That fateful Wednesday afternoon, after we got home from school, my father decided it was time to get our family out of town. The bank had just repossessed my little Mini Cooper that my parents had given me for my birthday, and my dad couldn't take anymore. My father never told any of us where we were going that day. He just kept repeating for us to get into the Hummer and so we finally did as we were told, and we didn't ask any questions. We sat quietly and rode away in silence. Even my mother didn't question him. We never told anyone where we were going, because we didn't know.

After my father died we realized that no one would come looking for us. Eventually, people would discover that we were missing, but they wouldn't have any idea which direction we went, so they wouldn't even know where to go to search for us.

As I sat there under the big tree at the fire camp remembering the past two years, my disturbing thoughts were interrupted by the loud commands of the fire captain. He was assigning sets of crews to head out to contain the raging fire that was now taking over a large percentage of the thick Idaho Wilderness Area. It was a desperate situation, the fire was late in the season, and most of the firefighters thought they were through for the year. We had to admire the dedication of each firefighter because they had a job to do and they were anxious to get it done. They were well trained and they followed through with their task with little instruction. The large masses of firefighters boarded several open camouflaged vehicles and quickly drove away leaving Clayton and I standing under the big Oak tree all alone. As we watched them drive away I had an odd feeling of separation anxiety, although I don't know why, for they had never even spoken to us. I guess it's the constant fear of separation that I have struggled with since my parents died.

After everyone was gone my little brother and I sat down under the big Oak tree and waited. We weren't sure what we should do. We were down from the mountain and we were safe, but we didn't even know where we were.

We sat quietly under the shady Oak tree for several hours, staying out of the way and waiting for some sort of instruction. Finally, the camp cook came out to where we were sitting and threw two camp sleeping bags down at our feet. Without saying a word he turned around and silently headed back toward his cooking tent. A short time later he returned with a small tube tent and sat it beside the two sleeping bags. "I've got some spaghetti and French bread made if you're hungry," He said gruffly as he turned and walked away. Clay and I looked at each other and shrugged our shoulders, then obediently followed.

Spaghetti sauce! Real spaghetti sauce made with real hamburger. It was delicious. We were the only ones left in the fire camp besides the cook. It seemed that even the fire captain had gone somewhere. So we enjoyed two large helpings of the cook's fabulous spaghetti and three pieces of his marvelous French bread along with two small cartons of fresh milk. The camp cook was a man of few words but he sure made a great meal. He left for a few minutes then he returned with a plate full of warm brownies. Melt in-your-mouth brownies! They were so good, maybe not quite as good as our friend Kennedy's brownies, but pretty close. For the first time in two years we were stuffed, and it felt amazing.

We helped clean up our paper plates and plastic silverware then we headed out the door to go back out to our tree. "Thank you for the delicious meal," I said to the cook as we walked out the door. For the first time since we had arrived at the fire camp, the cook smiled and nodded his head to us.

"Spaghetti with real meat sauce, French bread, fresh milk and warm brownies," I thought to myself. I knew that I would fall asleep thinking of my mother.

Clay and I climbed into the nice cozy sleeping bags and slept under the stars. We never even put up the small tent. Except for the faint smell of smoke from the distant forest fire, our camping spot near the tree was almost perfect.

I soon heard my little brother snoring in a calm restful sleep. I took a few minutes to thank the Lord for the day's miracles, and then I too went to sleep.

Before daylight we heard the roar of big trucks bringing in many more firefighters to head to the fire lines. Shortly after their arrival the fire captain had them corralled out under our tree and he was shouting out commands to organize each crew.

The cook had hash browns, scrambled eggs, bacon and toast ready to serve to the masses before they headed out to the fire. You had a choice between orange juice, apple or tomato juice. We ate breakfast with all of the firefighters, but we didn't talk to anyone. Then we cleaned up our trays and went back out to our designated spot under the big Oak tree. It seemed odd that no one spoke to us or even asked us our names. Within a few hours the crews were all loaded in trucks and headed on down the road. Again, we sat quietly and stayed out of everyone's way.

Everyday for seven days we would eat, clean up our trays then go back out and silently sit under our tree. The only communication we had with anyone was the smile and nod from the camp cook after we thanked him for each meal.

On our eighth day at the fire camp a man with a big dog drove into camp and went over to visit the cook at his tent. The man left his dog outside the tent and told the dog to stay. The dog did just as he was told. He was very well trained.

When it was time for lunch Clay said he wasn't hungry. He stayed out under the tree and sat quietly. When dinnertime came, Clay again said he wasn't hungry. I was starting to worry about him because it wasn't like Clay to miss a meal. I didn't know what was going on in Clay's head, but

I was sure he must have been getting hungry by then. So, I fixed him a paper plate with a roast beef sandwich, potato chips, an apple and a carton of milk and took it out to him. Clayton quickly ate every single bite, than told me thanks, and leaned back against the tree.

A short time later, right before dark, the man with the dog came out to our tree with a plate full of warm chocolate chip cookies that the cook had baked for us. As the man approached our tree his dog ran up to Clayton wagging his tail as if to say hello, but Clayton was terrified of the dog. He started hitting at him and shouting for him to get away. At first I was really surprised by Clay's actions, and then I realized the dog was a big black German shepherd mix. It looked just like a black wolf.

I apologized to the man for Clay's behavior. "He really is afraid of dogs," I said. The man shook his head up and down pretending to understand. He commanded his dog to follow, and then he handed me the cookies and went back to the cook's tent. By the time the man and the dog had left Clay was shaking all over. I told him, "Clay it's all right, the dog is gone," but he couldn't stop shaking.

As we lie there in our sleeping bags that night, I knew Clay was remembering the wolves from up on Moon Mountain. It had only been a year since he was surrounded by an angry pack of wolves while he was fishing out near the stream. I know he will never forget the evil piercing eyes of that big black wolf as it snarled and crouched towards him. The giant wolf was the alpha male, the leader of the pack. The infuriated wolf stood only inches from my brother, ready to attack, and I was forced to shoot him with my dad's old shotgun. It stills sends cold chills up my spine to even think of that horrendous night over a year ago. It was a living nightmare, because late that night as Clay and I tried to sleep, the wolves returned. We knew they had come back to avenge their leader's death. The large pack of wolves surrounded our cabin pacing in a hunting stance. They had come back for us. We felt we were safe as long as we stayed inside the cabin, but we still remained hidden, huddled together in the dark, covered up under a large quilt our mother had made.

From that night on, we were held captive by our fear of the wolf pack. We were afraid to venture very far from the cabin and whenever we went outside we always carried Dad's old shotgun.

As I lay there in my sleeping bag, in the open field of the fire camp, I could tell that Clay had finally calmed down and he had fallen asleep, so I went to sleep too.

The next morning the sun was shining brightly as we woke up and climbed out of our sleeping bags. It was our ninth day of staying at the fire camp. I watched as the man and the big black dog got in a car and slowly drove away. He waved to us as he drove off towards the highway.

Clay walked with me over to breakfast after he saw the man with the dog leaving the camp. He must have felt it was safe again to go back to the cook tent. Neither one of us talked about the black dog nor the angry black wolf with the evil looking eyes. We just went to breakfast.

Around two o'clock in the afternoon, that same day, a man came over to our tree and asked us if we would be interested in getting a ride down to Boise. Of course the man had no idea we were from the Boise area, he was just offering us a way to get out of the fire camp. He said, "There will be a truckload of tired firefighters ready to return home if you want to ride with them." He then asked, "Is there anyone you would like to call to meet you when you get to Boise?"

We had been down from the mountain for nine days and this was the first person that had ever talked to us. I thought for a minute, my parents were both gone, so the only phone number I could even remember was my Grandpa Richardson. My grandpa! Could I really talk to Grandpa? I tried to hide my excitement. I didn't want this stranger to know how ecstatic I was. "Could I call my grandpa in Florida?" I slowly replied.

"Sure," the man said, "Call whoever you want to call, it doesn't matter to me."

My hands were shaking as the stranger handed me the camp cell phone. I excitedly punched in my grandpa's home phone number; the number I had dialed so many times before. I could hardly breathe. I would soon be talking to my grandpa and my grandma, the last of my family. The phone rang three times then the operator answered. I must have dialed the wrong number out of my nervousness I thought, so I hung up and dialed again, only slower that time. My heart sank because the operator answered again and this time I listened to what she was saying. She said, "I'm sorry but this number has been disconnected."

"No, No," I thought, "let me try it again." So I dialed it three more times but every time was the same. My hands were still shaking as I sadly handed the phone back to the stranger. "I guess there is no one for me to call," I said looking down at the ground.

"How old are you guys?" the man asked.

"Umm, I'm sixteen and my brother is thirteen," I said in a whisper without even looking up.

"Oh, O.K.," the stranger quietly answered. "Without any family we'll have to send you to a foster home until we can figure out where to send you. I'll tell the captain," the man said sympathetically as he turned to walk back to the fire captain's tent.

Clay and I just stood there in shock. "Foster home? We have to live in a foster home? No way," I thought to myself. "I'll have to figure something out, but our first task is to get beyond the mountains and get back to Boise."

We promised each other not to talk to any of the firefighters on the ride home. We were not going to let anyone know who we were or anything about us. That should be pretty easy because up until now, none of the firefighters had asked us a thing.

THREE

Within a half an hour we were climbing into a big open forestry truck with several of the firefighters, ready to head down to Boise. Clay and I let everyone else get in the truck ahead of us. We waited so we could sit in the very back of the large truck. There were probably twelve other guys sitting in the forest fire truck with us, but we sat clear to the back by the open door. Lucky for us the firefighters were tired, dirty and anxious to get back home, so none of them talked much. Most of them leaned their heads back against the truck seat and fell asleep.

As we headed to the gas station to fuel up the truck, I read a big sign on the side of the road, it read: Welcome to Grangeville. "So that's where we have been for the past nine days," I thought to myself. "The fire camp was set up near Grangeville, Idaho. Our family went to Border Days, in Grangeville almost every Fourth of July. Border Days was a three day festival full of family activities and rodeos. In fact it was the oldest rodeo in Idaho."

As thoughts of Grangeville ran through my head, I thought about my mother, I remembered how much she liked to go to Miller Hardware when we were in Grangeville. It was an old hardware store that combined unique antiques along with all of their new merchandise. It had been owned and operated by the Urbahn Family for four generations, since 1913. Mom said it was like taking a step back in time. It was the oldest business in Idaho County, and she loved going there every time we went to Grangeville.

There was also, a cool saddle shop called Ray Holes Western Store where they built hand-made saddles and other leather items that were sent all over the United States. Many of their specialty items were even exported overseas. My dad had bought two of our horse's saddles there. Our family thought it was interesting because Mr. Holes made everything right there, in his shop in Grangeville.

Realizing we were in Grangeville gave me a warm feeling of relief, and for a few seconds I forgot that Clay and I were all alone in the world. Grangeville, Idaho held wonderful memories for us. It stood for a happier time in our life, a time when we were secure as a family.

As we pulled out onto the highway my brother and I watched out the back of the truck. We had a perfect view of the scenery, it was awesome. It was quite an adventure going down the steep White Bird hill in the back of the huge forest fire truck. The incline was thrilling and fast and I counted three run-away truck ramps before we finally got to the bottom of the grade. It was exhilarating to watch out the back of the big opened roof truck and to feel the wind blowing on our faces. The truck rode kind of rough, but we loved it. We smiled at each other and hung onto the seats, as we bounced up and down in our seatbelts as the massive truck rambled on down the highway. We were going home and nothing could rob us of the joy of going home.

We got to the bottom of the mountain and crossed a high bridge and it wasn't long before we came upon the river. The river was on the right side of the truck. As we traveled beside the river we waved to some people floating down the river in rafts. A short time later we crossed another bridge, and came around the bend to the little town of Riggins, Idaho. The air got thicker with smoke the closer we got to the town. The smoke had kind of settled in-between the mountains, and it still remained hovering through the canyon. Then I heard one of the men say to the rest of the firefighters, "I'm sure glad we kept the fire away from this quaint little town, it would have been a disaster for all of the townspeople if it had ever reached them." All of the men shook their heads up and down in agreement then they leaned their heads back against the truck seat and went back to sleep.

I remembered the fire captain talking about Riggins back at the fire camp. "They must have successfully kept the fire away from the town," I thought.

The rolling hills looked beautiful, as we sped by on our way to New Meadows. We pulled into New Meadows for a quick rest break before heading on towards McCall. My brother and I stood close together, away from everyone else, so no one would ask us any questions. We got out, and we got back in without saying a word to anyone.

The road between New Meadows and McCall was crooked and steep but the driver took it slow and easy as the big truck struggled to climb the curvy highway up the mountain to McCall.

As we drove in through McCall my mind traveled back to days of the Winter Carnival with all of the ice sculptures. We always had to take lots of pictures of the snow statues, because Grandma Suzanne had loved every one of them so much. Again my mind drifted off as we drove through McCall. "Where are my grandparents? Did something happen to them too? Oh Lord please let them be alive. They are all we have left," I silently prayed.

The driver didn't stop in McCall he just traveled on through, then he turned to the right at the corner on Main Street and we headed out of town. We drove past Donnelly, Cascade, and Banks, and then we headed into Horseshoe Bend. I knew we were getting close to Boise, because we had traveled on this road so many times before with our parents.

As we started up the steep Horseshoe Bend hill my insides started to feel a little uneasy. We would soon be home, but where is home? Clayton and I didn't belong anywhere. We surely didn't belong in a foster home, but we had been gone for almost two years and I wasn't sure where to go. I was suddenly struck by the same reality that my mother had feared. We had lost everything; and our world as we had known it was gone.

As we got closer to town I realized we were almost to Beacon Light Road. Our family's house was a couple of miles down the road to the right. I started to panic. What are we going to do? Will anyone even care that we are back? I felt sick. I knew I needed to take care of Clayton, but who was going to take care of me? "Oh Lord I feel so alone," I silently prayed.

The big truck motored on down the road as the driver headed for town. Clay and I watched out the back of the truck as we pulled up to a signal and turned right on old highway 44. The driver then turned left on Eagle Road and headed for the freeway. He drove straight down Eagle Road for a few miles then we turned onto the freeway and headed in towards Boise. The closer we got to town, the sicker I felt.

I knew that Clayton was depending on me, because I was the big brother, but now that we were back in Boise I didn't know where to go. I fearfully prayed, "Oh Lord, please help me because I don't feel like the big brother, I feel like a scared, lost little child that knows that his mother will never come looking for him."

As we jostled on down the freeway the firefighters started to wake up and get ready to get out of the truck. It was frightening because nothing along this stretch of the freeway looked familiar to me, then I noticed a huge airplane taking off to the right of us and I knew we were out near the airport. "Of course, I know where we are," I thought to myself. "We are clear on the opposite side of Boise."

The driver turned off at the airport exit, and then he turned left at the signal and drove straight on down the busy frontage road that ran parallel with the airport runway. The big truck rambled into a large parking lot near the end of the runway, and stopped under a small tree at the back of the parking lot. The men stood up to get out. Clay and I got out first because we were in the rear of the truck, then one by one each firefighter grabbed his duffel bag and headed for the building. Even the driver got out and walked away and headed for the structure with the rest of the men. Luckily for us, everyone was tired from the long trip down from Grangeville.

No one even noticed my brother and I standing near the back of the truck. After they had all gone inside the building we started walking down the road. We walked casually at first because we didn't want to alert anyone of our leaving. There were so many cars pulling out onto the frontage road that no one paid any attention to us anyway, so we just kept on walking.

FOUR

We crossed the freeway at the airport exit because there were sidewalks for pedestrians to cross over the overpass. When we reached the other side we briskly walked down the hill until we found the first subdivision area and turned in there. There were lots of houses so we could easily walk through neighborhoods and not call attention to ourselves. I wasn't sure how long it would be before the truck driver would discover us missing and call the police. I couldn't believe we were hiding from the law. My parents would be so embarrassed if they knew we were running from the police. No one in our family had ever been in trouble with the police before. We had always been such a respectable family.

We hastily walked through the neighborhoods weaving in and out of the streets. It had been an hour or so since we had left the firefighters and yet we still had not seen any police cars. We knew we must keep careful watch though because if they found us, we would never be able to get away. Clay and I knew that we no longer had anyone to protect us or defend us. If we were caught they would take us away, no questions asked.

We had been walking at a fast pace, but it was starting to get dark by the time we passed the train depot and headed down the hill towards the park. I could see the Boise State University campus off in the distance, and I knew that Julia Davis Park wasn't very far away.

It was dark by the time we finally reached the park and it was kind of eerie walking through the tall trees that late at night. I had always loved the park, but it was a little surreal being there after dark. It had been a long day and we were ready to hide someplace and rest for a few hours. We were both getting hungry, but we had no food or anything to drink. We didn't have any way to buy food, because we hadn't had any money for almost two years, but we hadn't needed it before now. I walked over and sat down next to the old band shell facing the river, and Clay slid in beside me. It was pitch-black where we were sitting, but we felt it would be a good place to spend the night.

I had just closed my eyes when a passing vehicle startled Clayton and he elbowed me to wake up. Within a few seconds we saw spotlights shining on all of the trees and bushes. Soon teenagers were running in every direction. The policemen with the spotlights got out of their cars and started hollering at the kids to get out of the park. The teens were running everywhere, but luckily for us, none of them were running in our direction. The cops finally had them all corralled and peacefully led them back to their cars to leave. About fifteen minutes later everything was silent. They were all gone, the kids and the police.

When our hearts started beating again we decided it was time for us to hide somewhere else. We cautiously walked over to the bridge and climbed under the cement encasement. There was a dirt area just large enough for the two of us to sit. So, we silently sat down and leaned our heads back against the concrete sides and fell asleep.

FIVE

We woke up at daylight the next morning to the sound of rain pelting on the bridge over our heads. "Looks like it might rain all day," an abrupt voice said from the other side of the bridge. "You kids are new around here, aren't you?" the man said.

"I guess so," I timidly replied. "But how did you know that?" I questioned.

"Cause you're sleeping in old Hank's section," the man warned sternly.

"Oh, I'm sorry sir, we just got back into town, and we didn't know where to stay, and this looked like a safe place," I quickly explained.

"Sir?" the man said, "No one has called me sir for a very long time." The man looked at me confused and hesitantly said, "The name is Russell, Russell Albertson, you know like the store." Then he firmly asked, "Hey, what are nice kids like you doing staying under a bridge? Why aren't you home living with your family?" he demanded. "Are you run-a-ways?"

"No sir," I said sadly looking down at the ground. "It's a long story, but we're not run-a-ways." I closed my eyes hoping this man wouldn't turn us in to the police, and I shook my head and said, "We would never run away from our wonderful family." I went on, "I guess you might say they ran away from us." Then Clay and I stood up to leave, "It's been nice talking to you sir, Mr. Albertson, but we'd better go."

"Hey wait," the rough voice said, "Hank's not coming back. You're welcome to stay in his place if you'd like." He went on, "You seem like nice young boys and you don't seem like you would be much trouble."

"Thank you Mr. Albertson, but we have been gone for almost two years and we have people we need to see," I answered.

"Two years?" the man questioned. "That's a big part of a life for young men like you." The man sadly went on, "I haven't seen my family for almost twenty years. When my wife died, it almost broke my heart, I wanted to die too. So, I woke up one morning a few days after her funeral and I took my two daughters to my sister's house and never went back. I'm sure my daughters hate me after all of these years." The man looked kind of distant as we went on, "My girls should be in their early thirties by now. I think about them every single day." He looked directly into my face and said, "I wish I had done things differently with my life. Most days I get so lonely, but you can never go back once you mess everything up."

I stared at the man who lived under the bridge, and then I asked, "How long have you been here under this bridge Mr. Albertson?"

"Hank and I moved here from Oregon over nineteen years ago. We had to move around a little though, we couldn't stay in one spot for very long or the police would get upset with us, but we always came back here to our bridge. If we were too cold we'd stop by the rescue mission to warm up and eat hot food and spend the night." Russell went on with his story, "Hank and I met over in Oregon right after his wife divorced him, and we caught a ride to Boise and we've been here ever since." Then he sadly went on, looking out into space as if he were in deep thought, "Hank was like a father to me. He helped me to stay alive all of these years. I'd share with Hank and he'd share whatever he had with me. That's what friends do for each other you know?"

The old man got real quiet and he softly said, "Two days ago Hank wouldn't wake up, he must have died in his sleep." Then Mr. Albertson looked at us with huge tears streaking down his dirty face, "No one even cared but me. I rolled him out by the side of the bridge and then I hid and I cried. It wasn't long before some runners spotted him and soon two men from the morgue took him away in an old white van." He went on, "He was my best friend you know? He was my family." He looked up at us as he sobbed uncontrollably and he said, "Living under a bridge is no place for nice boys like you. When the rain stops you boys go on and find those people you haven't seen for the past two years."

I felt so sad for Mr. Albertson, but there was nothing I could say that would help him. I just looked at him and nodded my head up and down.

A short time later, the rain did stop and we said goodbye to our new friend Russell Albertson and headed off down the greenbelt towards Eagle.

SIX

I had ridden the green belt so many times with my friends, Michael, Duke, and Jonathon, that I knew if we stayed on the greenbelt we could walk all the way to Eagle Road.

It was much slower walking than it was when we rode our bikes, but at least we couldn't get lost as long as we followed the path. We were a long ways from Eagle, but following the green belt was the only way I knew for sure how to get all the way across Boise. We probably wouldn't ever see any police cars either, so I felt we'd be safer staying off the roads for as long as possible.

The rain that had fallen earlier kept a lot of people from walking or riding bikes on the greenbelt that day, so we passed very few people along the way.

My feet were really starting to hurt from walking so far in my dad's old boots. We were both extremely dirty and worn out and Clay and I had the same clothes on that we had been wearing for the past two weeks. We must have been quite a sight, clomping along in our old worn out shoes and boots. I looked over at Clayton and realized how seriously unkempt he looked. He was wearing one of my dad's old dirty white tee shirts that he had put on a few days before we were rescued. I could almost laugh, if it wasn't so sad. Then I looked down at the worn out old sweatpants he was wearing; they had belonged to my mother. They were at least six inches above his ankles because he was so much taller than my mother had been.

After two years, we had worn out almost every piece of clothing that our mother had stored in the clothes chest, up at the cabin. I had worn Dad's clothes, Clayton had worn mine and now Clayton had even chosen Mom's sweats.

As I sat there studying my handsome little brother, I noticed that his hair was a filthy sandy blonde color and matted and tangled and pulled back in a ponytail. He had my mom's olive tone skin and jade green eyes with dark black eye lashes. He had straight white teeth that hadn't been brushed since the morning we left the mountain ten days ago, and as I stared at my little brother resting over on a park bench, I noticed how much he was starting to look like my dad. Clayton was handsome and tall and he had the same honest baby face that my father had. My heart wanted to break as I looked at my poor innocent young brother and thought of all that he had been through in his short thirteen years. Yet he never complained. He trudged along beside me in his filthy old tee shirt, my old tennis shoes with no laces and no socks, and my mom's worn out old gardening sweats.

I had not looked at myself in a mirror for a long time, I was afraid of what I might see. The bathroom mirror up at the cabin had been broken for several months, and we hadn't had any reason to clean ourselves up anyway, because we never saw anyone. Now that we were back in town I really hoped we wouldn't run into anyone we knew, because I realized my clothes too were tattered and worn, and my hair was matted and dirty and almost down to my waist.

I was hungry and scared and I had no plan of action, but my unfailing little brother just trusted me completely. The only place I knew we could go was toward the town of Eagle, so that's where we were headed.

The greenbelt didn't seem quite as wonderful as it did when I was with my friends. It's a long walk from Julia Davis Park all the way out to Eagle Road. We were tired and very hungry because we hadn't eaten since lunch the day before at the fire camp. But we kept on walking, because I knew we would eventually end up on Eagle Road. Once we got to Eagle Road it would still be several miles down Eagle Road before we reached our old property. Even then I wasn't sure what we would find once we got there, but we had nowhere else to go.

We walked quite a few miles without stopping, and when we reached Eagle Road we turned right and started heading towards Beacon Light Road. The traffic was fast and heavy with people heading home from work. Many people stared at our odd looking mountain attire, our filthy appearance and our dirty matted unkempt hair. We couldn't stand the disgusted stares that people passing by were giving us, so we kept our heads down and our eyes focused on the shoulder of the road and tried to mind our own business.

We were aware that we were several miles from the place we had last seen the firefighters, but we still kept a constant watch out for police cars. I knew that at least three patrol cars had already passed by and they didn't seem to pay any attention to us. Apparently, we weren't breaking any laws by being dirty and unkempt.

I was sure that by now, we were probably far enough away from the area where they would have been looking for us. It had been almost twenty-four hours since we walked away from the fire center, so they would have a hard time finding us, and besides not one person even knew our names.

We stopped for a quick break and we sat down on the grass in front of an Albertson's store. Clay and I kept our heads down looking at the ground so we wouldn't call attention to ourselves. Every time we dared to look up, we saw the sneers on the faces of the people as they left the store parking lot.

We were tired and starving and wondering where we were going to hide for the night, when a blonde lady in a light blue car drove up beside us and rolled down her window. I was almost afraid to look up to see her face, but she held out her hand to give me something, so I reached out my hand to her to be polite. The woman looked me right in the eyes and smiled, and I smiled back at her. She was the first woman to smile at me since my mom died, but it didn't make me feel happy, it made me feel sad. She then shoved a paper in my hand and said, "Remember God loves you." Then she drove off down Eagle Road towards Boise. I was stunned by what the lady had said to me, because that was the last thing my mom had said to us in her goodbye letter. I was hesitant to see what she had given me, but when I opened my hand I saw a crisp ten-dollar bill. The lady had given us money. I had to choke off the deep emotions I was fighting. We must have looked like street people to her. "Oh Mom I'm so sorry," I quietly mouthed. Then I remembered the time when Duke and Devon's dad had given money and food to a guy standing out on the corner at a Winco store. I had a strange feeling come over me, as I recalled what that young man had said to us when my friends and I took food and money out to him that day. He said, "I never thought I could ever be this hungry."

My heart sank as I realized Clayton and I were now that hungry, and through a stranger's charity the Lord had provided us a way to eat. I closed my eyes tightly and silently thanked the Lord for his unfailing generosity.

Clayton and I walked into the Albertson's Food Store and bought two protein bars, two apples, two bananas, and a package of imitation sliced cheese and two small cartons of milk. We were starved, but we needed to save some of the money because we didn't know how long it would be until we could eat again. Several store employees glared at us and persistently followed us up and down the aisles everywhere we went. They wouldn't let us out of their sight. We could tell they didn't trust us. So, we didn't talk to anyone. We just got our food and left the store.

We walked a little further on down the road and remembered that there was a small park right in the middle of town where we could sit down and enjoy our delicious dinner. It was almost dark, so the park was empty.

Marilynn J. Harris

We still had several miles to go before we reached the corner of Beacon Light and Eagle Road where our property had been. We were totally exhausted, so I knew we needed to find a secure place to rest for the night.

We walked down Eagle Road a short ways and came across an old boarded up farmhouse that didn't have any close neighbors nearby. We went around to the back of the old deserted building to find a place to sleep. The backdoor was gone, so we stepped inside and sat down right inside the old doorway. It wasn't a Marriott, but we were safe. Clayton fell asleep as soon as he leaned his head back against the wall. I stared out of the doorway into total darkness. I remember when I was little I was so afraid of the dark, but lately hiding in absolute darkness had become our good friend.

SEVEN

We woke up the next morning as the sun filtered down on our faces. We finished the rest of the imitation cheese slices and we each ate our banana that we had saved from the night before. It was early, but we were anxious to get going. There was very little traffic on the road at that time. We had no idea what time it really was, because we hadn't used a clock or a watch for months. We just knew it was daylight again, and it was time for us to be on our way.

As we got closer to our old neighborhood my heart began to race. We had no idea what we would find once we arrived at our old property. It had been two years since we had driven away from our family home. I was terrified of what we might find as we walked around the corner towards our old lane. Our beautiful home was still perfect two years ago when we drove away with our parents, but I did see smoke coming from the area of our house as we left, and then we heard a loud explosion.

I suddenly stopped, my fear had overpowered me, and my legs refused to move. I was afraid to go any further. We had talked about going home for so long, but now I was horrified at what we might find.

It was my little brother who then continued on, he was ready to go home. Clayton scurried about thirty feet ahead of me and then he turned and hollered for me to hurry up. As I came around the corner, I saw two large gates blocking our driveway; gates that had never been there before. They were solid, white metal gates and they were latched tightly with a thick chain and a giant padlock.

We quickly climbed over the tall solid fence and pounced down on the opposite side. We both stood in amazement as we stared at our once beautiful family property. The five-acre parcel was overcome with weeds and high grass. We cautiously walked down the old familiar lane that our family had once loved and adored. The white vinyl fences still rambled down each side of the lane, but that was the only thing that looked familiar to us. The weeds were so high, they grew well over our heads and we could not yet tell if the house and barn were still standing.

When we got to the end of the lane we were surprised to see that they both still stood unharmed, but every single window and door was boarded up with huge pieces of thick sturdy plywood. The boards were securely mounted with giant screws so that no one could enter or even see inside.

Clay and I walked over to the barn and discovered that it too had been boarded up.

We walked around to the back of the house and discovered the pool and Jacuzzi were drained and they were both full of dried leaves and weeds. It was obvious that no one had lived at the house for a long time. We could tell that everything was neatly put away and hidden before it was boarded up. Only Mom's old greenhouse was left unattended, so that's where we would stay. We were home! We were finally back home.

The fruit trees were plentiful with an abundance of growth. Apparently, fruit trees didn't need a lot of attention. So, we gorged ourselves on pears, apples, and peaches. It felt so good to be home.

That night we bedded down on the dirt floor of Mom's greenhouse and felt happier than we had in months. I carefully took my mom and dad's wedding pictures out of the inside of my worn-out filthy flannel shirt. Then I arranged them up against the end of the greenhouse wall where we could easily see them.

I was pleased with myself that I had gone back into the cabin and retrieved the pictures off of the fireplace mantel, as we were being rescued during the forest fire. I had grabbed the pictures and hidden them inside my shirt as Dallas and George the two helicopter pilots were pulling Clay up to safety. The pictures had been safely hidden there ever since.

As I lay there on the ground listening to my brother's light snoring, I looked up at the tattered pictures of my beloved parents and I mouthed, "I love you infinity." I again choked back the heavy emotions I was feeling and I was ready to fall asleep.

As I lay there in the dirt, I noticed the light on the barn came on and lit up the entire backyard. It reminded me of the bright moon on Moon Mountain that was at that moment shining down on my beloved mother's grave. I fell asleep thinking of my beautiful mother, she would be so proud of us for getting back home.

A few minutes later, I woke with a start when I remembered the barn light worked on electricity. I instantly sat up, that meant the power was on. I jumped up and ran outside and ran over to the horse's water faucet and opened it until the water started running out. "We have water," I yelled. Clay ran out of the greenhouse half asleep, and when he understood what I was saying we both jumped up and down pouring cool fresh water over our heads and arms. We had water.

We fell back to sleep that night thinking we were in heaven; fresh fruit, a greenhouse to sleep in and running water, what more could two teenage boys ask for.

The next morning we overslept, but we knew it was ok, because after two years we had finally reached our destination, we were home.

We got up and we took turns taking long cold showers under the barn water faucet. It felt so good to be clean. We just showered in our clothes so they would be clean too. We didn't have anything else to put on anyway, but at least we felt cleaner.

Each day we could feel the mats washing out of our hair. We didn't have any soap, but we had lots of fruit and we rubbed it into our hair then washed it out clean. We knew that a lot of shampoos that people buy at the store have fruit scents in them so we used what we had. Clay and I both knew we needed to try to be the cleanest that we could be, before anyone saw us. When you live alone on a mountain no one really cares if you have huge mats in your hair or not, because no one ever sees you, but down in Eagle, Idaho it was not acceptable. So we worked hard to clean off the two years of grime that we had accumulated.

EIGHT

We had been home several days and it felt great to be safe on our own property again, but bright and early on the fifth day we heard strange sounds coming from the front of the house. It was barely even daylight yet and we couldn't quite see where the sounds were coming from. It sounded like a power drill. Then I realized someone was taking down the plywood sheets off of the doors and windows. We sneaked around the side of the house, being careful to stay hidden and out of sight. I froze abruptly in my tracks; because from where I stood I could clearly see down our family's lane, and the padlock had been removed from the gate and the gate stood open wide. Someone with a key was in our yard. My heart sank. Our house must belong to someone else.

Marilynn J. Harris

Clay and I stood still wondering where we should run and hide, when a man with a baseball cap came walking around the side of the house and startled us. Clay quickly ran to left side of the house and I took off down the lane.

We were both scared to death until the man with baseball cap commanded us to stop. I paused and stood completely still, my heart stopped beating for several seconds, because I recognized that voice. I instantly turned around and ran across the yard and flew into the open arms of my grandpa. "Oh Grandpa, Grandpa, Grandpa, you're alive," I shouted. "We tried to call your phone number and your phone was disconnected and we were afraid something had happened to you. What are you doing here?" I asked as I buried my face into his shoulder, trying not to act like a big baby. Before Grandpa could answer I saw Clayton and Grandma Suzanne coming around the corner of the house, walking arm in arm.

The four us stood huddled together, holding on to each other, silently weeping in the middle of the tall weeds of our once beautiful front yard.

After several minutes of hugging each other, Grandpa said, "Let's go sit over on the porch where we can talk. The plywood can wait." As we sat down on the railing Grandpa Bill started to explain why he was there. He said, "I received a long distance phone call from the state police yesterday. They said a sixteen year old boy and his younger brother had tried to call our home phone number on a cell phone from a fire camp in Grangeville, Idaho a few days ago." Grandpa went on, "A man at the fire camp said he had allowed the sixteen year old boy to use his camp cell phone and the phone number that he had called had been disconnected.

44

The man told the police that the boy was so determined to reach us, that he had dialed the number over and over again several times." Grandpa Bill continued, "After the boys left the fire camp, the camp cook convinced the other man to trace the number the boys had been calling. Apparently, the men knew that the boys were calling someone in Florida." Grandpa explained, "They finally decided to try to reach the Florida State Police and have them track down the people who had recently had that phone number. It took them a couple of days to track us down." Grandpa smiled, "The men told the Florida State Police that the two boys were very polite and they seemed like nice young men that had just been down on their luck. The two men told the police they really wanted to help the boys find there way home."

Grandpa grinned and said, "We knew it was our grandsons as soon as they described how polite you both were." Grandpa looked over at me and said, "We came as soon as we got the call from the State Police. We were so elated to finally hear something after all of these months that we dropped everything and we caught the latest flight out of Miami last night and flew all night to get here." Grandpa said, "We had planned to fly into Boise then come out to Eagle and get the house ready, so it would be back in order when your family got home.

We knew you were heading towards Boise in a forest fire truck because that is what the State Police had told us when they called." Grandpa grinned as he shook his head and said, "We planned to hire the private detectives again so they could find you, but I should have known that you boys would figure out a way to find your way home." Then Grandpa buried his face in his hands and he sounded tormented and he said, "We have been to Boise so many times in the past two years and we

45

have felt so helpless, but we never stopped praying for you." Grandpa looked up, "When the state police called us yesterday we knew our months of praying had been answered." He went on, "The strange thing is we just had our home phone disconnected a few weeks ago." Grandpa shook his head, "Your grandmother and I had traveled back and forth to Boise so many times in the past two years that we decided we didn't need a landline anymore, we could just use our cell phones."

Grandpa shook his head and said, "I'm sorry Will, I knew that would be the number you would try to call. That's why I left it connected for so long." He went on, "I thought about disconnecting it several months ago, but I couldn't get myself to do it. We had been searching and wondering where you were for almost two years with no word, so we thought it was finally time to have it disconnected."

Grandma Suzanne then said, "I knew in my heart that you would one day come back home." Then Grandma continued, "We had the house professionally boarded up about a year and a half ago so that no one could get in. We cleaned out the refrigerator and all of the food cupboards before the house was sealed up." She went on, "Then we left the electricity on to keep the heat and air conditioner on so nothing would freeze or get too hot.

We wanted to make sure the house would be ready for all of you when you came back home." Grandma told us, "After the house was boarded up we always stayed in a hotel in downtown Boise when we came to town. We drove out to this property whenever we were here, but nothing had ever changed, so we knew that no one had been back." Grandma continued, "We had posted your pictures all over the Internet and newspapers for several months after you first disappeared. We even hired private investigators to help track you down, but they found nothing. It seemed as if you had just evaporated into thin air." She shook her head and said, "Not one person had reported seeing any of you, and we didn't even know what direction to search. We never even found the Hummer anywhere."

Grandpa spoke sadly as he held Clay on one side of him and me on the other, "It is so hard to lose your whole family and just have them vanish without a trace in one night." Grandpa said, "We knew within twenty-four hours of your disappearance that something was wrong. Your friends at school went to the principal when you didn't show up for school the next day.

Hailie told Mr. Ryan that you had text her the night before and said your family was going away for a few days, but Michael and Duke argued that you wouldn't leave without telling them you were leaving. So, they all knew something was wrong. Your friends called us five times a day for the first several months after you first disappeared." Grandpa shook his head, "They just couldn't believe you were really gone."

Grandpa continued, "When they first went to Mr. Ryan he had called your house and all of the cell phone numbers that he had been given, but no one answered so he called me in Florida. I knew that there had been something wrong with your father because he kept avoiding me," Grandpa said. "He stopped taking my calls at his office and he hadn't talked to your grandma for several weeks before your disappearance." Grandpa looked at the ground, "We didn't know about his corporation collapsing until after we arrived in Boise two days after you were gone."

Then Grandma Suzanne timidly asked, "William, where are your mom and dad?" She was afraid of the answer, but it was obvious to both of them that Clayton and I were on our own.

I looked at my grandma with tears in my eyes and cautiously said, "They're both dead Grandma. I'm so sorry, but they're both gone."

My precious Grandmother nearly collapsed as she ran over to my Grandpa and buried her face into his chest while they both trembled and gravely cried together. My heart was breaking as I stood there and watched my grandparents. I dreaded telling them the horrendous happenings of the past two years. Even sitting safely on the porch railing of my family home, the events of the past two years did not seem real to me.

As much as I dreaded telling them, I knew that I had to explain everything that had happened, so I somberly began to disclose the events that led to my father's death. I said, "Dad drove us up to our cabin on Moon Mountain to get us away from all of the humiliation and scandal going on about his corporation. Many of the company's employees were angry and very hostile about losing their jobs. They had worked for the company for many years and when they lost their jobs, they lost everything. Dad was trying to protect us. Mom said he feared for our safety." I covered my face and continued on, "He knew we would be safe at the cabin. We had food, water and shelter and no one knew where he had hidden us.

He drove us up to the cabin late one Wednesday evening right before Halloween two years ago." I went on, "It was raining so hard that night that the rain was running over the rain gutters and flooding down the face of the mountain. It poured down rain all night long, and early the next morning Dad tried to sneak away and head back to town before any of us were awake." I slowly continued, "I woke up just as he was leaving. I helplessly ran after him in my shirtsleeves and bare feet. It was still raining so hard that he couldn't hear me hollering at him as I slipped and trudged through the deep mud trying to catch up to him." I closed my eyes trying to escape the overwhelming sorrow that I felt as I once again recalled all of the events of that hideous morning. I looked up at my grandparents and continued, "I watched in horror as my dad lost control of the Hummer in the slippery mud. He went over the side of the mountain, then the Hummer rolled several times and burst into flames." I slowly continued, "As the Hummer rolled down the mountain it created a massive mudslide taking the old road with it, along with most of the mountainside.

Apparently, Dad had planned to leave us hidden on Moon Mountain for a few days until things calmed down, but with so much rain the night before it was too slick for him to get back down the old road." I covered my face with my hands; I couldn't bear to look at my grandparents anymore. "The Hummer rolled to the bottom of the mountain, and then Dad was completely buried under huge masses of mud, rocks, and trees," I whispered. Big tears rolled down my face, but I still couldn't look at my grandparents. I'm sure what I was telling them was far worse than anything they had ever imagined. I kept my hands covering my face for a few minutes but I could hear my grandparents sobbing across from me on the other side of the porch.

"Oh Dear Lord," I prayed silently, "I feel like everything is happening all over again." As I sat there on the railing, I kept my head buried in my hands but I soon felt my grandmother's loving arms wrap around my shoulders to comfort me.

She whispered into my ear as she held me tight, "Oh my poor babies," she said as she sobbed. "My poor precious grandsons, I can not believe the torment you have been through." Then she lightly rocked me in her arms, just like she did when I was little. She quietly whispered, "It's all right now, it's all right. You're home now and Grandpa and I will take care of you. The Lord has brought you safely back home to us."

As I looked up I realized that Grandpa was hugging Clay while Grandma held me. Clayton my tall, handsome sibling, my brother, my helper, my friend; I would have never survived without my amazing little brother, my flawless, trusting companion. My father was right. Having a little brother really was a special gift.

I took a deep breath, and then collected my thoughts for a few seconds and I decided I better tell my grandparents about the death of my mother. I'm sure they were dreading hearing about her death almost as much as I was dreading telling them, but they needed to know. So, I took another deep breath and continued on, "Mom lived on the mountain with us for almost a year, but she got weaker and weaker every day. She had been having some problems even before we left. She had an incident at church, just a few weeks before we disappeared." I rubbed my hands over my face and went on, "She had fainted during church service and she wouldn't allow anyone to call an ambulance. She convinced all of us that she was just exhausted." I shook my head, "She told us after we arrived on the mountain that she had been having a hard time eating anything because of all the stress with our dad's company. But even after we arrived on Moon Mountain we had to force her to eat. She seemed to be alright for the first few months, and we talked a lot, but once we had been at the cabin for a while she started getting very withdrawn and afraid. She completely stopped eating or drinking any water." I shook my head and continued on, "Her fear of coming back to town got worse and worse every day. She missed our dad so much and she knew that her old life was over. We tried to help her, but she continued to get more disturbed about everything no matter what we said." I was crying uncontrollably by then, "She became so thin and frail and she soon couldn't even walk by herself. We knew she needed to be in a hospital, but there was nothing we could do for her."

Then Clayton began to talk and he said, "Mom just got worse everyday until she could no longer even get out of bed. She needed to see a doctor and Will and I could not take care of her." Clay covered his face and wept, and then he continued on, "Mom died last summer and Will dug her grave and we buried her on the top of the mountain."

Again my bewildered grandmother held me close and whispered, "I am so sorry Will. You boys have been through so much."

We all sat silently for several minutes trying to collect our thoughts. Then my Grandpa broke the silence when he stood up and said, "Well we can continue talking later, but we'd better get to work if we're going to get all of the plywood down by this evening."

It was then that I asked him, "Is the house all right? I can see the outside is fine, but wasn't it mostly destroyed?"

"Oh no," Grandpa said, "It had some smoke damage outside the kitchen where the barbecue caught on fire, but we had the clean up people take care of everything right after it happened." He went on, "So, except for a few smoke stains by the patio doors, the house is just like it was when you left it."

I questioned, "The barbecue caught on fire?"

"Oh yes," Grandpa said, "Someone left a can of wasp spray on top of the barbecue and they left the barbecue turned on high and it got too hot and it exploded." Grandpa went on, "The alarm system notified the fire department immediately so the firemen kept the fire under control and there was very little damage to the house; mainly just clean up from the smoke."

My mind was fuzzy. "Someone had turned the barbecue on high and it exploded?" I thought. "That must have been the smoke and the explosion we heard as we drove away that Wednesday afternoon." My thoughts raced, "I guess we'll never know for sure what happened, but why would the barbecue even be turned on that day?"

I shook my head then walked over to help Grandpa and Clay who had already started to remove the first sheet of heavy plywood off of the front door.

The plywood was really heavy, and it took all three of us to get the huge boards down from the front door. I wasn't sure if Grandpa could have even gotten them down alone. It was a good thing we were there to help him. I'm sure Grandpa would have ended up hiring someone to take it all down for him if we hadn't been there to help. The plywood had been up for a long time and it was in no hurry to come down.

Grandpa Bill slowly removed one long screw after another until all of the boards were carefully released. A professional builder had put up the plywood for my grandparents several months ago, so the boards were determined to stay in place. The builders had done an excellent job of keeping everything locked up tight and everyone out of the house. The large pieces of plywood must have discouraged anyone from trying to get in because nothing appeared to be damaged on the outside.

After we took the plywood down from the front door my grandmother went inside and started straightening things around. I wanted to go inside so badly, but I knew we needed to help Grandpa with the plywood. Therefore, Clay and I continued to work until several sheets from the front of the house had been removed.

Grandma Suzanne had started opening up all of the windows in the front of the house as soon as we got the plywood removed. A short time later she stuck her head out the front door, "Come in and eat," she shouted. "I'm sure you are all starving. Grandpa and I stopped and picked up a few groceries on our way out to the house this morning, and luckily we bought enough food for all of us."

My brother and I then slowly walked in the front door of our family's beautiful home. Our house, a place we had not entered for over two years. So much had happened to us in those two years that our brains were on overload. Our mother thought our house had been destroyed and yet here it stood. Our home, our place of belonging, a place I had visualized for so long, but thought I would never see again.

I cautiously walked in peering into every room. The front room was empty, just as we had left it. My father had sold all of the furniture to try to generate some income. My grandparents stood in the hallway quietly watching us; they were wise enough not to ask us any questions. They knew there would be time for questions later. We slowly made our way to our mother's revered kitchen and sat down at the places that Grandma had prepared for us. Clay sat in his regular chair and I sat in mine. My grandpa sat in my dad's chair and Grandma sat in my moms.

It was eerie sitting in our family kitchen remembering how much my mother had loved her beautiful gourmet kitchen. She had designed every single detail of the kitchen just exactly the way she wanted it to be. It was haunting for me to actually feel her absence.

Grandma had fixed us scrambled eggs with cheese, fried bacon, and warm homemade biscuits with jam. We had orange juice and of course fresh ice-cold milk. Grandpa finished his coffee as Clay and I ate the last of the biscuits and jam.

Then Grandma poured a hot cup of coffee for Grandpa and one for herself, and then she sat down at the table. "Why don't you boys go check out the rest of the house before you get started working on the plywood again," Grandma suggested.

I looked at her and nodded. She must have realized how anxious we were to make sure everything was all right after being away for so long.

Clay quietly walked into his bedroom, as I walked on down the hall to mine.

The door to my room was closed and I quivered as I slowly turned the knob to enter into my room. A wave of nausea came over me for one short second, as I slowly opened the door and looked into my colorful blue and orange bedroom. Everything was exactly as I had left it two years ago. I smiled at the huge Bronco Head painted on the end of my bedroom wall, it matched the Bronco Head that was sewn on my bedspread. I gently touched each signed football sitting precisely on their stands. Then I carefully traced the outline of the blue turf on the poster above my desk. Except for a little dust, everything was perfect. I bounced down on my bed with my head on my pillow and I felt a hard lump under my right shoulder. I reached up to see what was making the lump on my bed and I discovered my cell phone. It was right where I had thrown it two years ago after I sent a text to Hailie.

I lay there on my bed staring up at the ceiling for awhile, wondering about the many changes that had unavoidably taken place while I was away. I thought about Hailie, Duke and Michael and my old school. I had not gone to school for almost two years, what grade would I be in I wondered?

I reached into my back pocket for my old wallet and I pulled out the worn picture that I had been carrying of Mom and Hailie standing in the kitchen right before we had disappeared. "Hailie, my girlfriend, my best friend. I wonder if she even remembers me," I thought to myself.

My deep thoughts were interrupted by the sound of the screw gun diligently working to remove the large sheets of plywood. "It was time to get back to work," I thought. "Grandpa and Clayton needed my help."

The three of us worked all day until we had removed every sheet of plywood from every window and door around the house. We left the barn boarded up, because we were all getting worn out and there was nothing in the barn anyway. We would tackle it another time.

While the three of us had been working on the plywood, Grandma had been inside dusting and changing the sheets on every bed. She had washed the insides of the cupboards and cleaned and vacuumed every single room. The refrigerator had long been empty but now it was spotless and cold. My miraculous grandmother had also fixed a delicious dinner of meat loaf, canned corn, warm rolls, and mashed potatoes. Sometime during the day, in her spare time, she had also created one of her luscious award winning apple pies from the apples off of our trees. My mom was a great cook, but no one cooked with her heart and soul like my grandma did.

We were stuffed, exhausted, and ready for a good hot shower. I walked into my bedroom and opened the dresser drawers and discovered all my clothes folded neatly and organized just like the day I had left them. We're home. In just sixteen days I have gone from being trapped on the top of Moon Mountain in a forest fire, to the quiet safety of my Bronco bedroom. I grabbed a favorite pair of pajamas out of my top drawer and headed for the shower. I hadn't had a long hot shower since the night before we left home two years ago.

I stood under the sizzling hot water letting it penetrate clear to my bones. It felt so wonderful I thought I might never get out of the shower again. My long hair felt thick and heavy as it hung down my back. Never in my lifetime had I ever wanted a long, blonde ponytail; but for the past several months it had become a part of the person that I was now. I got out of the shower and tied my long, clean blonde hair back into a band to keep it out of my face. I put on my ankle-high pajamas and then stared at myself in the mirror. For weeks I had studied my little brother's appearance, but I had neglected to see myself.

Mom had accidentally shattered the only mirror in the cabin months before she had died. She was sick and frail and had lost her balance, and when she tried to catch herself she hit the mirror with her hairbrush in her hand, and the mirror shattered all over the bathroom floor. So I hadn't looked at myself in a mirror for several months. My features seemed so much older than I remembered. My chin seemed squarer than it used to be, and my face showed signs of a light beard. I had my father's eyes, but they looked sadder than I remembered his eyes looking. I then glanced down at the huge scar that ran down from my elbow to my wrist. "A lasting trophy from my struggles with the mountain," I thought. I covered the scar with my pajama top and headed out to check on Clayton and Grandma and Grandpa. As I walked out to the kitchen I could hear my family laughing while they each drank hot cocoa with big marshmallows floating to the top. My family, it felt so strange to have a family again, but it was a happy kind of strange.

Grandma fixed me a cup of steaming hot cocoa with extra marshmallows then set it down in front of my place. I quietly took my chair and sipped the delicious warm chocolate. Grandma knew just how I liked my hot chocolate. It was excellent. I sat there quietly listening to the innocent chitchat between Clayton and my grandparents. I hadn't heard Clay talk that much since we left home almost twenty-four months ago. It was comfortable just to sit back and listen to the family chatter. I didn't need to say a thing.

I studied my grandparents as they sat and talked easily with Clayton. My grandpa Richardson was tall, slender and very physically fit for a grandpa. His hair was thick and full, and silvery-white, and he had the same handsome baby face as my father and my brother. He looked much younger than other men did that were his age. Even after all of the heartache of the past two years, he still had that bright gleam and sparkle in his clear blue eyes.

In all of my lifetime my grandma Suzanne had always looked exactly the same. She was stylish, graceful and gentle, and when I was twelve years old she was voted Mrs. Florida, in a beauty pageant in a contest with other ladies her age.

Suddenly, my grandpa stopped laughing and he got a more serious tone to his voice. He said, "Grandma and I have decided we need to live here in Eagle with you boys. We know some people who want to lease our house in Florida and we can stay here to keep you boys settled in your own family home." Grandpa looked down at the table and then he said, "We have all been through so much in the past several months, it's time we start getting our lives back in order." He continued, "The payments on your family's property were behind when your family left." He then talked to Clay and I as if we were adults and said, "I had my accountant bring the taxes and the house payments all up to date. I made arrangements with your father's bookkeeper to send any bills to my accountant in Florida. He has been paying all of the bills for both our house in Florida and your Eagle house ever since you left." Grandpa looked over at my grandma and shrugged his shoulders and said, "We were trying to alleviate some of the stress from your father and also make sure the house was all right when your family returned home." Grandpa then said, "My accountant has been handling all of your family's personal finances too, whenever something needed to paid, he just took care of it. All of your family's finances are up to date."

My grandmother then reached over and covered my hand with hers, and she looked straight into my eyes and said, "A house is just a building unless it has a family to make it a home." She smiled at me with glistening tears running down her soft face and said, "Our house in Florida has become just a building, this must now become our home."

I stood up and wrapped my arms around my precious grandmother's neck. I quietly whispered so that everyone could hear, "I always knew you and Grandpa were brilliant." With so many other unanswered questions going through my mind, at least now I knew we could stay in our family home.

I then headed off for bed and Grandma looked at my high-water pajama bottoms and said, "Well, one of the first things we need to do is go buy you boys some new clothes. I think you have each grown at least four inches since you left two years ago."

I laughed at Clayton's short pajamas, as we both strolled off to our bedrooms feeling the weight of the world had been lifted off of our shoulders. When I reached my bedroom I tossed Clay a pair of my pajamas from out of my dresser. They would probably fit him perfectly. He was almost as tall as I was but I still out-weighed him by several pounds.

As I lay there in my bed that night, between my fresh clean sheets, and my incredible Bronco bedspread, I couldn't help but praise the Lord for the past sixteen days of miracles.

Sometime during the night Clayton had his reoccurring nightmares, and he woke up and silently crept into my room with a handful of blankets under one arm and his pillow under the other. He quietly made a place on the floor, at the foot of my bed, and then he fell sound asleep, just like he had done so many times before in the past two years up on Moon Mountain. This small troublesome gesture was never a problem for me. My poor little brother had been through so much confusion in his innocent young lifetime. I knew that some day he would again feel secure enough to sleep all night alone in his room, but at this point in his life he continually required the assurance that I was still close by if he needed me.

Marilynn J. Harris

NINE

As we woke the next morning we could hear the bustling of Grandma fixing breakfast in the kitchen. She made waffles with warm syrup and fresh peaches off of the peach tree. They were delicious! Apparently, while she had been waiting for Clay and I to wake up and eat, she had been busy making a giant grocery list of everything we needed to fill the refrigerator and the pantry.

I heard Grandpa on the phone in the other room talking with a local gardener making plans to get the yard and fields back in order. Grandpa grinned when he saw me walk in. "We'll have this place back in shape in no time," he stated. "We'll need some help at first, but then I think between the four of us we can keep this property looking the way your mother would want it to look," he said winking one eye.

Then Grandpa called someone to make arrangements to lease out their house in Florida. He made a second call to one of his lifelong friends, and he asked him to hire a moving company to sort out their house and put everything into a huge storage unit and then have a cleaning service get the house ready for them to lease. He told the man he would come down in a couple of days and decide what needed to be moved to Idaho. I overheard him tell the man he needed to stay in Eagle for a day or two to get our family's property back in order before he could come to Florida. Then Grandpa turned away from me while still talking to his friend, "Yes, yes, that's right Suzanne and I are staying here with the boys. Yes, we are going to live in Idaho." He quietly said, "This is what we need to do, I'll tell you all of the details when I see you in a few days. The boys have been through so much and they need to be in their own home." The man on the other end of the phone talked and my grandpa just listened and then he finally said, "Thank you Frank, I really appreciate it. I'll talk to you later." Then they both hung up. Grandpa never looked at me again. He just stared at the wall for a few seconds then walked into the other room.

I slowly went back into the kitchen feeling a little guilty because my grandparents were giving up so much. I walked over to my grandmother who was joyfully adding items to her growing shopping list. I watched to see if she showed any signs of misgivings, but instead of acting sad she started singing. I was taken by surprise by her enthusiasm and delight, and then I had to smile when I realized what my grandmother was singing. She sang, *"I've got peace like a river, I've got peace like a river, I've got peace like a river in my soul..."*

Evidently moving to Idaho was something my grandparents had thought about for a long time and they truly were excited about it.

A huge grin covered her face as she looked up and saw me watching her. She smiled at me with so much love in her expression that I wanted to cry. Again she came over and hugged me until I thought I might stop breathing. Then she said, "Hey go find something to wear, because we're going shopping."

I hollered at Clayton as he was finishing his last bite of waffle. I told him, "I'll get you something to wear out of my drawer." I walked into my bedroom and grabbed a pair of Levi's and a shirt out of my dresser and threw them on my bed for Clayton, and then I headed on down the hall.

I cautiously walked towards my parent's bedroom. Their door was closed but I slowly opened the door into their charming, impeccable fortress. I had always loved their bedroom. It looked like a room out of an enchanted castle. It was elegant, flawless and beautiful. My mother's favorite color was dark-green and everything in the room showed off her gifted designing nature. A heavy sadness fell over me, and I felt the loss of my parents more in that room than in any other room in the house. That was their room, their private refuge from the outside world. It now seemed dark, unapproachable and empty.

I slumped down on the loveseat at the far end of the room and I felt a hollow loneliness that would have easily overpowered me if I allowed it to. Again my heart began to break, being in their bedroom made me aware that the changes that had happened to us in the past two years were permanent. My parents were never coming back. Clayton and I would be forced to live the rest of our lives without them.

I buried my face in my hands and I wanted to scream, but my painful thoughts were interrupted by a gentle tapping on the bedroom door. "William, are you in there?" Grandma softly said.

"Yes Grandma, I'm in here," I said. "I was just getting some of Dad's clothes." I quickly ran over to the closet and grabbed a pair of sweats and I reached down and got the first pair of tennis shoes that I found. I then headed out of the bedroom door and closed the door tightly behind me and I didn't look back.

I put on my dad's sweats and tennis shoes and headed for the car. I never even looked at myself in the mirror to see what I looked like.

By the time I got to the car I was thoroughly overcome with anguish and fear of leaving the house. I slowly got into the rental car that my grandparents had rented at the airport when they had first arrived, and then we drove down Eagle Road to go out shopping. I had not been out in public or seen anyone that I knew for over two years. For some reason I feared seeing people that I hadn't seen since I disappeared. I sat quietly in the backseat with my head leaned over towards the window watching everything as we passed by. I knew the world had gone on without us while we were away, but I wasn't sure I wanted to know exactly how it had gone on.

When we were up on the mountain with no hope of coming home, we knew that life as we had known it was gone forever, and we were forced to accept it. Now that we had actually returned home my brother and I didn't know exactly where we fit. Most of our life had been centered around our family, friends, Dad's company and our school; but as we drove down Eagle Road that day I felt empty inside because we no longer had any of those things.

The first store we pulled into was Kohl's. It was right down the road from our house so we didn't have to go very far. Grandma thought she could find most everything she wanted to find for us in there. Then she planned to go buy groceries after we were done buying clothes. Grandpa pulled into a parking space and my heart began to sink because I knew I had to get out of the car and walk into the store.

Both Grandma and Grandpa were out of the car and waiting at the front entrance, but Clay and I just stared out of the car windows with the doors still closed. I finally became aware that Clayton hadn't moved either and when I looked over at him I could tell by his expression that he must have been feeling the same panic that I felt. We then gave each other a reassuring nod then opened the doors at the same time and climbed out into the bright sunshine.

We walked slowly towards the sliding doors, keeping a careful watch for any familiar faces. I can't explain the strange emotions I felt. For months I had dreamed of being home again, but as we walked through the Kohl's department store that day I walked in total apprehension. Upsetting thoughts went through my mind, because the last time I went to the Kohl's store I was with my mother and my little brother and we were the wealthy sons of a prominent CEO.

I dreaded having to explain the terrible problems that had occurred since I'd been away. I hadn't seen anybody for the past two years and I didn't feel like telling my harrowing story to anyone. I walked around the store keeping my head down and trying not to make eye contact with any of the people.

My grandmother quickly picked out jeans, shirts, shoes, underwear and pajamas then we headed for the register to pay and leave the store.

Grandma told us, "This will get you off to a good start, and then we can sort through all of the old clothes and see what else you might need." Luckily, we got to the car and never talked to anyone except the store clerk.

As we pulled into the grocery store parking lot Grandpa could tell by the way we were acting how much anxiety we had about going shopping again. He suggested that the three of us go buy ice cream cones while Grandma got what she needed at the store. My grandma loved shopping so she was delighted to get us out of her way for awhile. Grandpa dropped her at the front door of the store and told her we'd be back shortly. Then he drove on down the street to buy us ice cream.

As much as I loved ice cream, I really wasn't very hungry. I bought one small scoop of Rocky Road just to please my grandpa. Then the three of us sat silently over in a corner of the small ice cream shop eating our ice cream until it was time for us to go.

Within an hour we picked up Grandma and all of the groceries that she had bought and then we quickly headed on home.

When we arrived at our driveway we saw yard workers everywhere. They were busy mowing, weeding and pruning bushes. Two men had already cleaned out the swimming pool and Jacuzzi and were already filling them full of chemicals and sparkling clean water. One man was checking the sprinkler system while another man mowed down the field with a large tractor lawn mower. We were amazed at how quickly the clean up crew could put things back in order. It was wonderful to see our property become the way it used to be.

About an hour after we arrived home a flower delivery van pulled up and a lady from the flower shop started hanging colorful baskets of flowers all around the porches like my mother had always done.

The deck and pool furniture were all gone because my father had sold everything to generate some money before he had taken us up to Moon Mountain, but even without any furniture it looked great. The yard crew had everything looking flawless and neat before they left that day.

After all of the workers were gone Grandpa grilled hamburgers on the barbecue. My grandparents had bought a new barbecue shortly after the other one had burned up. Clayton and I set up a card table and chairs out on the deck, while Grandma made a potato salad, a leafy green salad, and frozen peas and onions, to go with fresh-squeezed lemonade. We had strawberry shortcake with real whipped cream for dessert. It was great.

Although, we had a lot of things we needed to discuss we didn't talk much that night. Grandpa and Grandma were quiet after dinner so we watched football for several hours and ate popcorn and pretzels then went to bed.

It was pretty late by the time I finally got into bed, but I had a hard time falling asleep. For some reason I didn't feel as content as I did the night before. I looked up at my big Bronco clock that was hanging above my doorway and I knew that I had been tossing and turning for several hours. I quietly got up out of bed and was careful not to bother Clayton who was again sleeping on the floor at the foot of my mattress. I then walked out onto the porch through my outside bedroom door. I walked across the deck and sat down on the top step next to the railing and I stared out into the darkness. It was a beautiful September evening. Idaho often has summer-like weather clear up until the middle of October. I was home and I was safe with my grandparents and we had plenty of food to eat, but my mind still raced with so many unanswered questions. "How will people accept our return home?" I thought. "People were so angry with my father that he felt he needed to hide us away on an isolated mountain just to protect us from everyone. Are they still angry with our family?" I wondered. "Will they take their anger out on my brother and I or my grandparents?" I asked myself. I bowed my head into my hands, "Oh Lord what if no one wants us here?"

When we were trapped up on the mountain I never worried about all of the anger that people had towards my father. I knew that we were isolated and they could never hurt us way up there on Moon Mountain. I never felt the problems that my dad had with his company had anything to do with us until now; but now that we were back home we are all that is left of our family for people to be angry with. Although, it is not my battle I am still my father's son. I covered my face again, "Oh Lord I am so afraid. You have brought my brother and I so far, but this confusion with my father's company has destroyed so many people." As I sat there on my porch step I just wanted to scream. Sitting there in the darkness, feeling all alone, I knew exactly how my father must have felt when his whole world fell apart and everyone turned against him. I was so tired of my heart hurting all the time. I missed my parents so much, I decided to walk out to the greenhouse and talk to my mom and dad for awhile. I stumbled along the driveway in my bare feet crunching through rocks and dirt until I finally came to the door of my mom's beloved little greenhouse. I gently opened the door and sat down on the dirt floor and started talking to their pictures as if they were sitting there with me.

Mom loved her greenhouse so much and it honestly felt like she was right there reassuring me and telling me that everything was going to be all right. I carefully reached over and took their pictures off of the end of the greenhouse wall. My parents, my father and mother, my heritage, even death could never take that away from me. I hugged their pictures close to me as I stared out into the darkness for a few more minutes, then I yawned and I knew it was time to get some sleep. As I went back inside and climbed back into my bed I looked at my clock for one last time and I saw that it was 4:18 in the morning, almost daylight up on Moon Mountain.

TEN

The next morning as I exhaustedly crawled out of bed, I overheard Grandpa ordering tickets for the four of us to fly back to Florida to get all of their things in order.

Grandma said, "We won't be gone long so just pack enough clothes for a couple of days." She continued, "Mainly, just the new things we bought and your bathing suits."

A few hours later we locked up the house and we were off to the airport.

As we were riding up the escalator at the Boise Airport, I kept looking around hoping I wouldn't run into anyone my family had known. As I glanced down into the giant lobby by the main entrance, I saw my eighth grade English teacher, Mrs. McKinney as she was quickly walking into the airport terminal through the sliding glass doors. I still wasn't ready to see anyone that I knew even someone as nice as Mrs. Carol McKinney. I didn't say anything to my grandparents or Clayton about seeing my teacher. I just emptied my pockets at the check-through station and got ready to board the plane for Florida.

Our family had traveled all over the world, but as often as I had flown this time seemed different. My insides had butterflies and I felt a little queasy. Between my nerves and the lack of sleep, I felt terrible. I buckled my seatbelt and leaned my head back against the seat to try to relax and I closed my eyes. I didn't wake up until three hours into the flight. I never even woke up when we landed in Salt Lake City or when we took off again. Grandma said I was just exhausted from so many changes in my life and I needed to rest. I never told her that I was awake most of the night thinking and fretting about everything.

September is a beautiful time of year to visit Florida. It is not as hot as it is in the mid-summer time. Our family always loved going to Miami that is where Clayton and I were born. We lived there for the first few years of our lives. It was hard for me to believe that my grandparents would no longer be living in Florida. They had lived in their same house ever since I could remember and I loved going to visit them and walking up and down the white sandy beaches. The beaches stretched for miles and miles in both directions. "How could they give up everything?" I questioned. The ocean view from their back deck was unbelievable. I used to sit and watch the waves for hours at a time. It was so peaceful, but it would soon be gone.

We arrived in Miami around 8:30 that evening so we took a taxi straight to a hotel. My grandparent's house was being emptied out and cleaned up to be leased to one of their friends. We ate a late dinner at the hotel then we headed back to our room and decided to turn in early. I knew my grandparents had a lot to do while we were in Florida and they had many huge decisions to make.

The next morning my grandfather took off before breakfast and left Clay, Grandma and I to hang around the hotel pool for awhile. Clay and I swam while Grandma sat in a lounge chair and read. It was great not to have to think about much of anything. Around noon Grandpa came back to the hotel to have lunch with us. He seemed a lot more pensive than he had before he left that morning. He told us that he had met with his banker, his lawyer and his accountant. He had a lot of arrangements he needed to get taken care of and he felt it might take them a few more days to get things in order than he first thought. He said, "I have set up an appointment for all four of us to meet with my lawyer tomorrow morning because there are several legal things that we need to discuss."

Later on that afternoon Grandpa and Grandma went off alone for several hours and left my brother and I in our hotel room to watch television. They told us we could order room service if we needed a snack. We always loved ordering room service, so we called to order a big container of nachos and two giant Dr. Peppers.

It was almost dark by the time our grandparents returned from their errands. I could tell my grandma had been crying throughout the day. She tried to hide it, but I knew this was going to be a tremendous change for both of them. They had to move clear across the United States away from all of their friends, their church, and their beautiful Florida home.

Grandma forced a pleasant smile and said, "We went and picked up Grandpa's Mercedes so why don't we all get around and go out for pizza."

"It would feel good to get out of the hotel for a few hours." I said.

Around 10:00 we went back to the hotel and got ready for bed, because we had a big meeting with Grandpa's lawyer first thing in the morning. My dad had several friends that were lawyers, but this time it was different, this was business and I could tell that my grandparents were both really concerned about the meeting.

When we arrived at the law office the next morning we discovered that Mr. Jenkins, Grandpa's lawyer, and Mr. Brooks, Grandpa's accountant were both there. They were friendly and nice and asked if Clayton and I would like some orange juice and a sweet roll before we got started. We politely declined and I instantly got that sick feeling again. I suddenly wanted to take off running because everyone was acting so strange, including my own grandparents.

Mr. Jenkins then cleared his throat and said, "Dr. Richardson has asked me to go over some of your family's legal affairs with you." He then opened a file with a stack of papers which were sitting on his desk. Mr. Jenkins went on, "Will, Clayton, I have asked Mr. Brooks to join us today because for the past two years he has been handling all of the finances for your family's home and properties." Mr. Jenkins spoke very candid as he continued on with the discussion, "I understand that you boys have lost both your father and your mother in the past two years, is that correct?"

I nodded and quietly answered, "That is correct sir."

"Is there any way we can prove that your parents are both dead?" Mr. Jenkins solemnly said.

I looked over at my Grandma Suzanne who was softly weeping as she kept her eyes to the floor. Then I looked at Grandpa and he nodded, "Go on William tell them everything that you know."

"Well Mr. Jenkins," I stammered, "I watched as my father's big Hummer went over the side of the mountain and burst into flames. That happened the second day that we were up at the cabin, almost two years ago." I sadly went on, "Then I saw the mountainside completely bury him and his vehicle leaving my mother and my brother and I trapped up at our cabin on Moon Mountain." I then looked at the floor and sighed before saying, "As for my mother, she died almost a year after my father died and we buried her up next to where our cabin used to be." I shook my head and continued, "We saw the cabin and everything around it burn up in a forest fire a few weeks ago. Didn't we Clay?" Clay nodded his head up and down and then looked downward at the floor. "Luckily, Clayton and I were rescued by two helicopter pilots that were scouting out the fire or we would have burned up too," I concluded.

Mr. Jenkins went on, "Therefore, you really have no definite proof that your parents are dead?"

I looked up quickly with a shocked expression on my face, "I never knew I would need proof that both of my parents died and left us all alone." I continued with some hostility in my voice, "My brother and I were devastated when we lost our parents. We did everything that we could to figure out how to survive on our own." I tried not to get angry with Mr. Jenkins but I was having a hard time. "Our parents had always taken care of us; I was only fourteen years old when my dad died."

I covered my face to keep from crying, then I took a deep breath and bluntly responded, "After both of our parents were gone we were so heart broken that we could barely keep on going we wanted to die too. I had tried to hike down the mountain alone a few months before Mom died, but I got lost in the dense forest and discovered that I had been walking around in circles." I slowly continued, "I had walked all day and when it started to get dark I panicked, because I couldn't tell where I was the forest on our mountain was so thick. Even in the daytime the sunlight barely came through the thick trees. I knew I needed to figure out how to get down from the mountain because our mother got more and more depressed with each passing day. She would barely eat anything and we were afraid to leave her alone. Clayton stayed with her and I took off by myself. I wanted to get down from the mountain and get her help, so she wouldn't die, but it didn't work," I said half whispering looking down at the floor.

Clayton could tell I was really getting upset, so he stood up and started talking trying to clarify what had gone on and he said, "A few weeks after mom died we tried to hike out together. We thought at that time all we needed to do was hike down the mountain until we could find a trail or road or something." He looked over at me and said, "But that didn't work either." He let out a huge sigh and then said, "Will lost his footing on the loose mountainside and he fell several hundred feet down the mountain and was injured really bad." Clayton shook his head and said, "He got a big gash on his head and a deep cut down his arm and he lost a lot of blood. I was really scared. He was unconscious for several days and I was afraid he was going to die too and leave me all alone at the cabin." Clay looked at me and shrugged his shoulders and went on, "When he finally got better we were afraid to try to leave again, we couldn't take a chance on anything happening to either one of us."

As Grandma listened intently to what Clay was saying she jumped up from her chair and ran over to question me, "Will you were unconscious for several days and you almost died?" She then looked over at Grandpa and shook her head back and forth and her voice quivered as she said, "Oh Bill our boys have been through so much I just can't bear it." She covered her face with her hands and fought back tears as she returned to her chair and hesitantly sat down.

I then lifted up my sleeve and showed them my long scar. I also, pointed out the faded scar that ran across my forehead. I guess Grandma hadn't noticed my wounds until then. If she had she never mentioned them or asked me about them. So much had gone on in the past two years and we hadn't really told anyone anything that had happened to us until now.

Mr. Brooks, the accountant, then interrupted our conversation and said, "I'm so sorry to hear about all of the tragedy your family has been through, but as you know I have been taking care of your father's business affairs since your family disappeared two yeas ago." He went on, "I am happy to inform you that all of your father's affairs are in order as far as I can tell, including all of his insurance policies." We all remained silent as he continued on, "Because of the large amounts on your father and mother's life insurance policies there is a written clause stating that in the event of their deaths the beneficiaries must show proof of their deaths by presenting a death certificate."

The room remained silent as he continued on and said, "That is why Mr. Jenkins is asking you so many questions about their deaths. To have a death certificate you must have a coroner examine the bodies and decide the approximate time and cause of death."

I suddenly jumped up out of my chair. "So that's what this meeting is all about," I shouted. "You want to dig up my mom and dad to see if they are really dead?" I covered my ears I couldn't listen anymore. We had finally made it down from the mountain and they want me to go back up there to see if my parents are still dead. "No, no, no," I shouted in my head. "This can't be happening."

I had completely tuned everyone out, but I could still hear several voices talking at once, shouting all around me. I could hear Mr. Jenkins talking above the rest of them. He was saying something about how much of my grandparent's money had been paid out to keep my father's affairs in order while we were away.

"This is all about money?" I quietly said to myself, I hadn't even thought about how expensive everything had been for my grandparents. "Money," I thought shaking my head, "I can't believe everything is always about money." Loss of money is what got us trapped up on top of Moon Mountain in the first place. I placed my head in my hands, "Why is life so hard?" I questioned.

My poor grandmother just sat in her chair and cried uncontrollably. I'm sure listening to all of this was thoroughly breaking her heart.

Finally, Grandpa walked over to me and put his hand on my shoulder and made me look up at him. "William," Grandpa said, "It's not about the money to us. We would have spent everything that we had to get your family back home safely. Your grandmother and I feel that we need to get the bodies of your dad and mom down from the mountain so we can have a proper funeral service and bury them in a cemetery." He went on, "We also, need to contact your mother's sister, Margaret, who lives in Baltimore and let her know about your mother's death."

I can't explain it, but looking up at my beloved grandfather that day; it seemed that everything he said to me made sense. He was right. Of course we needed to bring my parents down from the mountain. I would have never left them all alone up there, if I could have brought them back home with me. So, I gave my grandpa a weak smile, and shook my head up and down letting him know that I agreed.

Mr. Brooks, Grandpa's accountant spoke up again, "I have gone through all of the legal papers that your father's accountant had sent to me two years ago." He went on, "I have the plat maps with the legal descriptions of a cabin property clear up near the Wilderness Area, and I have paid those taxes along with all of the other taxes that your parents owed. However, the name Moon Mountain is not written on any of the property documents. I can't seem to find the Moon Mountain property that you keep talking about. Did your parents own two mountain properties?" Mr. Brooks looked at my grandfather, "I'm sorry Bill, but I never paid any taxes for the Moon Mountain property."

I instantly looked up at Mr. Brooks and said, "No, you wouldn't find it written on any of the maps. Moon Mountain was just the name my mother named her mountain the very first night we were up there. That was our family's private name for our mountain cabin."

Mr. Jenkins and Mr. Brooks looked at Grandpa with questionable expressions on their faces. Then Grandpa confusingly looked at me and stated, "I always thought that was the name of the mountain range where your cabin was located and we had no idea where that was."

"No, my mom just called it that because the full moon seemed so close up that high on the mountain," I thoughtlessly told the men as my mind drifted back to a happier time in my life. "My family once loved our cabin property so much," I remembered. "We thought it was the most wonderful place on earth." Again my thoughts drifted off as I sat there in the lawyer's office that day, hiding silently inside my own private world. After all the tragedy that Clayton and I had lived through on the mountain it was hard for me to remember why our family had ever loved Moon Mountain in the first place, but I knew that we had.

The three men were still talking, but my thoughts kept drifting off and I again tuned everyone out. I had a hard time paying attention to everything they were saying. I just wanted to escape. I didn't want to listen.

They caught my attention again when they said, "Then it is decided; we can make arrangements for Dr. Richardson and William to go back up to the property in a rescue helicopter and bring Clint and Marci back home."

I instantly felt sick again and started to break out in a cold sweat, I didn't want to go back up to the mountain, but I didn't know how to get out of it.

Then Mr. Jenkins looked over at me and said, "You say two helicopter pilots found you? Do you know the names of the two pilots that saved you?"

I had to think a minute, "I don't know their last names I just know their first names were Dallas and George." I thought for another minute and then I said, "They were the scouts for the fire camp, and they were the first ones that were sent out to check on the exact location of the fires." I saw Mr. Jenkins writing everything down. Then he turned to Grandpa and Mr. Brooks and I heard him say something about Grandma and Clay could remain at our house in Eagle until we returned from the mountain.

"Oh great," I thought to myself, "Clay gets to stay home and I am being forced to go back up on the mountain. I don't want to do this, but there is no way they are going to allow me to get out of it." I got a little braver and I spoke up, "I'm not sure if we would ever be able to find where my father was buried anyway. Even if we did find it he was buried under piles of rocks, dirt and trees. In fact, I'm not sure if we could even find Moon Mountain again because of the fire. I really doubt it would do us any good to even go back up on the mountain again, it may just be a waste of time."

Mr. Jenkins was not someone who took no for an answer. He asked me in a very forceful tone, "Well if they could find the mountain where the cabin used to be, do you think you could find where your parents are buried?"

I could tell they were not going to let me get out of going back up there. I let out a huge sigh and said, "I guess so. If we can find the location where the cabin was I know exactly where I buried my mother."

Grandma Suzanne walked over and put her arms around me and said, "Oh Will, I am so sorry. I can't believe you have to go through all of this again."

I nodded my head up and down without saying anything. "Oh Lord," I thought to myself, "I'm not sure if I can do this again. Why can't I just be sixteen and go to school and hang out with my friends like other guys my age?" I sat there quietly thinking to myself while every one else around me talked.

When the meeting was over Mr. Jenkins and Mr. Brooks stood up and first shook my hand then shook Clayton's hand. They were cordial and polite and treated us like we were adults instead of teenagers. My mind was on overload, I dreaded getting back into a helicopter and I definitely didn't want to fly back up to Moon Mountain, but I knew no one could find my parent's bodies without my help. My brain was screaming, "No I won't go back up there," while my mouth was saying to the two gentlemen, "Thank you, it was nice to meet you too."

We were all relieved to get that morning over with. After the meeting was over we went to one of my grandparent's favorite restaurants down on the beach. It was extravagant and relaxing. I had a giant shrimp cocktail with a cup of clam chowder and Clayton had his very favorite meal, lobster. It was a great ending to a horrendous morning. We then went back to the hotel to get our suits to go hang out on the beach for the rest of the day.

As hard as I tried, I couldn't get that appalling meeting with the lawyer and the accountant out of my mind, but I never mentioned it again and neither did anyone else.

That evening we had a light dinner down on the beach, and then we returned to the hotel to get a good night sleep. We knew that tomorrow was another day of big decisions. My grandparent's house was empty and it was time to go to the storage building and choose what they needed to have transported to Idaho.

When I went to bed I couldn't sleep. Every time I'd try to fall asleep I'd see my frail, dead mother lying on her bed. Beside her was my desperate little brother holding tightly to her hand. I had dreamed about my mother so many times since she died, and it was always the same dream. I pray that someday my mind will once again be at peace and I can dream the happy dreams of a normal teenage boy. For as long as I live I will never forget that horrible day fourteen months ago when I was forced to bury my beloved young mother. I had worked all day digging her grave in the hard, rocky soil, and now they were going to dig it up. It made me ill to think about everything. I turned over on my stomach and covered my head with my pillow, but I couldn't get those terrible images out of my head.

I couldn't get to sleep, so I turned over and quietly lay awake looking at the ceiling. I was so exhausted then I finally did doze off, but I was only asleep for a few minutes and I woke up screaming for my father. "Dad please don't go, come back, no please don't die. Please don't leave us." I felt so helpless, I felt like a little child again, "Daddy, Daddy, Daddy, please don't die, no Daddy no." I continued to shout until my grandmother came running in from the other room. Grandpa followed behind her and then he left to get me a sleeping sedative. Even though I was quite a bit bigger than my grandma was she sat on the side of my bed holding me until I finally relaxed enough to fall a sleep. "When will these terrible nightmares go away?" I muttered as I was falling asleep. "I want my mom and dad to be alive," I tried to shout, but the sleeping sedative had started to work and I slept.

We were all so tired the next morning that we slept in until after 9:00. Apparently, none of us had slept very well. No one mentioned my nightmares; we ate our breakfast in silence and headed out to my grandparent's house for one finale goodbye to their family home.

Their extravagant home looked so empty and alone with the furniture moved out. All of the floors and carpets were cleaned and shined just as Grandpa had requested. The windows and counters sparkled and shone from being washed and waxed by professionals. Their house looked brand new, but I knew they had built it long before I was born. I always thought it was the most beautiful house I had ever seen. I loved all of the windows and the open areas. It was enormous. Grandma showed little expression as she went from room to room inspecting everything for perfection. The cleaning service had done a great job; because Grandma soon gave it her sign of approval and without saying a word we locked all of the doors and windows and headed for the storage unit.

I could barely breathe, I was so sad as I sat in the backseat of the Mercedes listening to sounds of dead silence. I knew my grandmother had to be dying inside, but she never let on she just acted like this was what she needed to do. I knew how much she had always loved her house, and I knew that she would never live in it again.

The storage unit was several miles on down the road and we drove all the way there without anyone saying a word. My grandparents seemed relieved when we finally arrived at the huge gates of the storage place. Grandpa's friend, Frank had secured a large unit for them way down at the end of the buildings.

When we pulled into the unit Grandpa and Grandma were pleased to see that their friends Frank and Betty were already there waiting for them. Betty ran up to Grandma and hugged her for several seconds. Betty had tears in her eyes, but Grandma remained quiet and strong. It was overwhelming to me to see my grandmother's beautiful furniture piled end to end throughout the large storage unit. Grandma went through and chose each piece that needed to be sent by the moving van.

Grandma and Betty would often stop in front of certain items and discuss where something had come from or how heavy they would be to be transported.

Our house in Eagle, Idaho was not as large as their house in Florida had been, so Grandma knew she needed to get rid of a large percentage of her furniture. The ladies worked diligently all morning long and by lunchtime they knew it would take them at least another full day to get everything sorted out. They marked each item with a red tag that needed to be sent to Idaho. The items with a blue tag would be sold at an auction.

All of the changes in our lives just made me sick, but Clayton and I still helped our grandparents, by moving things around to help them get to each piece of furniture.

About 1:30 the six of us went down the street for a late lunch. We had worked hard all morning and Clay and I were really getting hungry. It was interesting to watch my grandparents sit and visit with their best friends. They understood each other so easily; they were all four so comfortable together. They just talked and accepted each other with such deep respect and admiration. I knew that their moving was going to leave a huge empty space in all four of their lives. We had known their friends, Frank and Betty since we were first born. They had always been there for our family.

So many things were going through my head, but I was just sixteen years old and I couldn't change anything that was going on.

Grandpa had to make plans to have his cars transported to Idaho. He contacted a big transport company that would be taking several other vehicles across America in a covered car carrier.

I watched him as he gently touched the 23 T-bucket that he and my father had built together when my dad was only seventeen. It made me so sad to watch my grandpa gently rub his hand across the smooth glistening paint. It was in mint condition. I'm sure it looks just as great today as it did the day they built it over twenty years ago. I could see the deep love and appreciation my grandpa had for the shiny blue hot rod. It was his baby, it was his pride and joy. They had built it out of some kind of hot rod kit, and my dad had told me many times how much fun they both had building a car together. Dad said it was probably the happiest memory of his youth. They worked on it most of my dad's senior year of high school. The next year Dad left for college and Grandpa kept the car in storage ever since, waiting for the day when my dad would want it back. It is a priceless reminder of a happier time in my grandpa's life. So, of course he would have it transported to Idaho.

They decided to sell Grandma's Lincoln because it was several years old and it would be cheaper to buy her a different car once they got settled in Idaho. It sure seemed like they had a lot of quick decisions to make. They finally decided that they would have to keep one of the storage units for at least a year, because there were too many decisions they needed to make in such a short time. They could return in a few months to finish up whatever needed to get done.

The next day we sadly said goodbye to Frank and Betty and we got on the plane to fly back to the Boise airport. It reminded me of when I was five years old and my dad had taken his young family and moved them all the way across the United States to Idaho.

I leaned my head back against the plane seat. I felt so grateful to my grandparents for everything that they were doing for us. I looked over at my grandma and smiled, and she squeezed my hand and smiled back. It was a long flight back to Boise, so I decided I might as well get some rest. I closed my eyes and soon fell fast asleep.

ELEVEN

When we arrived back in Idaho we were all tired and exhausted from the long flight from Florida and from making so many decisions over the past few days. It was evening by the time we finally arrived at our house in Eagle, and as the lights of the rental car shown upon the bolted gate we could tell something was wrong.

Someone had thrown eggs at the gate and into the front of the driveway. There was also a sloppy-looking hand painted sign that said *...Clint Richardson you killed my wife and you're going to pay for it.*

"Oh no, people must know we are back," I stated.

Grandpa and Grandma looked at each other with a questioning glance and then Grandpa got out of the car and carefully looked around before unbolting the gate. Then he slowly slid the gate open as Grandma, who was now in the driver's side, drove the car on through the open gate. Grandpa grabbed the offensive sign and abruptly locked the big gates back up before getting into the passenger side to go up to the house.

The automatic lights came on around the property and they completely lit up the entire yard area. It didn't appear that whoever had left the sign and egged the fence had come all the way into the yard. We each cautiously got out of the car, still watching all around us, and quickly took our luggage into the house.

When we were safely settled inside Grandpa checked every door and window of every room. Nothing was out of order. Everything remained securely in place and the security system was still on. After putting her suitcase in their bedroom Grandma headed for the kitchen to make us some hot chocolate and cinnamon toast.

As we sat around the kitchen table dunking toast into our hot chocolate, Grandpa finally asked us, "Do you boys have any idea who might have left that note and egged the front gate?"

Clayton spoke up first, "Grandpa we had no idea that the people from Dad's company were even upset with him." He looked over at me for reassurance, "Until we ended up trapped on top of Moon Mountain, and by then it was too late."

Grandpa then looked over at me. I sat silently thinking for a minute before I spoke up and said, "Mom did tell us that she had been getting some threatening phone calls from someone who said his wife was sick. She said the man called her Marci, but she couldn't recognize his voice."

Grandpa looked over at Grandma and said, "Suzanne, I know the boys have been through a lot, but I think it's time they know just how bad everything was after they disappeared."

Grandma wiped her hands across her face then nodded her head up and down that she agreed.

Grandpa left the room for a few moments, and then returned with stacks of newspapers that had been hidden away in my father's den for several months. He put the piles of papers down in the middle of the table for Clay and I to examine. Paper after paper had headlines with accusations about my father's company. They were all dated after our family had vanished. Each day would state someone's guess as to where our family had disappeared too. Most of the headlines were rude and slanderous.

As I stared down at the newspapers my heart began to break, "How could my family's perfect world get so messed up?" I thought to myself. "Why would people even say some of the things that they had said about us?" I sat there quietly trying to decide what I should think about everything. Then I looked up at my grandparents and asked, "What should we do? Are we even safe living here?"

Grandpa Bill looked me directly in the eyes and said, "William, people act crazy when they lose everything." He went on, "In the past two years I have seen young fathers who have lost their jobs, then they go on food stamps to feed their family, soon they lose their house, then they lose their integrity and eventually they lose their identity." He shook his head and half-closed his eyes, "So many people have a lot of experience and they have certain qualifications that they used for their job. But their experience and qualifications are no longer needed by anyone, because the job that they once did has been eliminated. So they end up feeling worthless, and they become completely different people than they once were." Grandpa put his elbows on the table and folded his hands in front of him, and he balanced his chin on his knuckles and said, "There have been so many people that have lost their jobs, and they may not find another job for over a year or longer. If they do get a new job they usually make a lot less money than they did before." He sighed, "It has been very hard on so many young families." He looked over at Grandma and said, "Grandma and I have spent a lot of our time filling food boxes for many of the families at our church in Florida." He went on, "Florida has had a really high unemployment rate for the past year or so, hasn't it Suzanne?"

"Yes," Grandma Suzanne added, "Many of our friend's adult married children have lost their jobs and they have been forced to move back home with their parents." She said, "Frank and Betty's son and his wife and two kids live with them; and Betty loves it."

"So, things really haven't gotten any better since we've been gone?" I asked.

Grandma slowly shook her head, "No, they haven't, but I am surprised that with so many people all over the country losing their jobs that anyone would still be angry with your father." She went on, "I am sure by now, that people have figured out the failure of his corporation had nothing to do with the way he managed it. Will, there have been hundreds of companies that have failed since your father's company collapsed." Grandma pressed her hands up over her ears and her cheeks as she went on, "Every one of those people are angry about losing their jobs, but they don't blame the company they worked for." She squinted as she said, "They know their companies didn't chose to go bankrupt."

"Yes, she's right William," Grandpa added, "That note left on the front gate for us this evening, doesn't really make much sense; but as far as being safe here, we will all be fine. I will call the police department and have them keep an eye on the house. The security system is on and everything is bolted tight, so I'm sure we will be safe for the night."

We went to our rooms feeling a little uneasy, but totally exhausted from everything that had gone on. I took a shower then climbed into bed expecting to have another night of tossing and turning and bad dreams, but instead I was out like a light until 8:00 the next morning.

I woke to the delicious smell of bacon, scrambled eggs and warm homemade blueberry muffins. Grandma was busy cooking in the kitchen, but I overheard Grandpa talking on his phone in the den. He was really serious as he said, "Yes, yes that's right the sign is written in blood." He seemed very upset, "Yes sir, I am a Doctor, I was a surgeon in Florida for thirty years, and it is definitely blood on the sign." He then looked up and saw me standing there, and he turned his face away from me so I couldn't hear what he was saying. Something was going on and he didn't want me to know about it. Within a few minutes Grandpa was off of the phone and he looked over at me with a very concerned look on his face. He hesitated, and then he decided he needed to tell me, "Will, I discovered this morning that the sign that was left on the gate yesterday was written in blood." He continued on, "I think it might be human blood and I have reported it to the police. They are sending out two detectives within the hour."

"What does that mean Grandpa, what is going on? What should we do? Clay and I haven't done anything to anyone, and we don't want to put you and Grandma in danger." I was rambling, "I can't believe this, does everybody hate us?" I bluntly asked walking around in a circle while shaking my head.

Grandma walked in from the kitchen and overheard us talking and said, "Why would everybody hate you Will, You are a wonderful person."

"I know Grandma, but so was my father," I told her sadly.

Grandma just totally ignored me and answered in her normal happy tone, "Well we'll all feel better after a nice warm breakfast." She looped her right arm in through Grandpa's arm and her left arm in through mine and led us gently into the kitchen.

Clay had just sat down in his chair as the three of us slowly walked to our places. Grandma was right, warm homemade muffins really did make things better.

Just as we were finishing breakfast the doorbell rang, and it was the two detectives from the sheriff's department. Grandpa Bill introduced himself; then he took them into the front room and showed them the messy looking sign that was left on the front gate the night before. The two officers wrote down several pages of information before putting the sign in a large plastic container to take to the police lab for examination. The first person they wanted to track down was someone who had worked for Dad, and had lost his wife in the past two years. They also, wanted to check with all of the neighbors because they suspected it was someone who could tell the house was lived in again. Probably someone who lived close, and was just driving by, and could see the lights on and the yard cleaned up.

Grandpa told the two officers, "The boys haven't even talked to anyone since they got back home, so no one even knows they are here." Grandpa continued, "I am a little worried because I am going to be out of town for a couple of days and I need someone to watch the house while I am away." He said, "I don't feel comfortable leaving my wife and my grandson alone with all of this going on. Do you happen to know anyone who I could hire to guard the house for a couple of days?" The detectives gave him the name of a policeman that was a friend of theirs that did private security work in his spare time. As the men were leaving Grandpa told them, "Thank you for coming by and I will contact the officer later on today."

As the policemen were leaving they warned us, "Remember to keep the doors, windows and the front gates padlocked until we can trace down the fingerprints and blood samples on the sign." As they shook hands with my grandfather they said, "Feel free to call us if you have any more questions or any further problems." Then the two men nodded their heads to Clayton and I and left to get into their car.

After the men were gone Grandpa told me, "Mr. Jenkins called me first thing this morning and he has made all of the arrangements for the two of us to fly up to Moon Mountain tomorrow morning with a recovery crew." Grandpa went on, "Mr. Jenkins found the two pilots, George and Dallas and they gave him the exact location where they had rescued you boys and we have the legal descriptions of the property. They were quite sure we could easily find where the property was located." Grandpa was so excited as he talked, "William, the two pilots said that they had also discovered a half-burned chrome spare tire rim in the canyon below where you and Clayton were rescued. They had noticed a bright reflection of something shining off of the bottom of the canyon, as they were checking for hot spots after that part of the forest had burned." Grandpa got excited, "They couldn't get real close, but they were sure it was the spare tire off of a large vehicle. Until we contacted them, they had no idea how it had gotten up there in the mountains." He went on, "Will, the search team is positive that with all of this information they have been given, they will be able to recover your father's body as well as your mother's grave." Grandpa Bill was so excited he had big tears running down his face, "Isn't that great? Will, we can bring both your father and your mother home."

All of the blood drained out of my face. I know Grandpa was still talking to me, but my brain had shut him out. "No, no, no more," my mind kept screaming. "Oh I feel sick," I thought as I took off running down the hall, but it was too late, and Grandma's muffins were so delicious at breakfast. I washed my face and I could hear Grandpa reassuring me outside my bathroom door. I looked at myself in my bathroom mirror and said to my ashen face, "What have I done to deserve this mess?" Then I remembered the saying that my dad had on a plaque above his desk in his office, it said: "The Lord never gives you more than you can handle." My father's job was very stressful and yet he firmly believed the words on the plaque. So, I wiped the shiny tears away from my eyes and said to my reflection in the mirror, "O.K. Dad, I'll bring you home."

TWELVE

Early the next morning, right around dawn, we boarded a big helicopter at Gowen Field and headed up towards Moon Mountain. The air was crisp and chilly but flying in a larger helicopter wasn't half as scary as the fire helicopter. The world looked fresh and innocent as I glanced down through the giant helicopter windows.

We were quickly flying over the houses and past the trees rapidly whirling to our mountainous destination. I personally had no idea where Moon Mountain was located, but the pilots navigated directly out of the city and promptly headed up towards the rugged isolated wilderness.

It wasn't long before we had entered into an eerie world of charred and blackened trees. Everywhere I looked the forest was gone. There were miles and miles of rolling black ridges where the majestic Idaho Mountains used to flourish. One black mountain looked just like another to me. "How would the pilots ever find our burned cabin location when every single mountain looked exactly the same?" Suddenly, the lead pilot turned around and told my Grandpa that the property was three miles off to the right, and we would be landing in the open area on the next plateau. Before the forest was destroyed there was no open area; but now that most of the trees were gone, there were open areas and plateaus everywhere.

All of a sudden I saw it and I watched in utter amazement as my family's private mountain came into view. Even through the soot and burned trees, I recognized my family's secluded hideaway. Although, it appeared completely different with all of the trees gone, I could still see the crumbled chimney, the cement perimeter foundation that once held the cabin, and the caved in cement food storage vault. That cement food vault had kept my brother and I alive for almost two years. We owe our lives to that vault.

As we carefully approached our mountain it didn't seem as sinister standing there all blackened and alone. It no longer stood proud and pompous; it seemed sad and defeated. I felt kind of bad for our mountain. The cabin was my family's own private paradise, and it was once my parent's ultimate accomplishment and pride. I had loved that mountain more than anywhere in the world. It was a magic place, a special time in my life, a time of closeness and being together with my family.

As we landed, a warm and comfortable feeling engulfed me, and I was so glad I had come back. I looked at my Grandpa and smiled, and then we both climbed out of the helicopter onto the crispy burnt foliage.

Part of the rescue team got out with us and headed over towards the damaged cabin and cement vault. The remainder of the crew stayed in the helicopter as it rose back into the air, and headed over towards the area that I had pointed to where I believed my father's body was located. Within minutes we could see a man off in the distance being lowered down the side of the mountain. He went down into the deep canyon where Dallas and George, the two pilots had spotted the shiny reflection of what was possibly the Hummer's spare tire. We stood in amazement as the man that was being lowered into the canyon signaled that he had already spotted the burned tire. The man soon dropped down out of sight and settled his footing on the bottom of the deep canyon ledge. Then we watched as they sent down instruments for the crew to help locate the Hummer buried deep inside the debris and canyon floor.

The rest of the crew that had stayed with us set out to uncover my mother's remains. We walked on past the destroyed cabin and walked over towards the area where I knew I had buried my mother, but everything looked so different. In my dreams, I always believed I could walk directly to her grave without any difficulty. But now as I looked around there were no longer any landmarks, the trees were all burned or gone and the ground had been totally burned to a crisp. The rocks that we had piled on top of her shallow grave were now covered with several inches of ashes and soot. All of the ground looked the same. The fire had been so intensely hot up there on the mountain, and the high winds had fanned the flames so much, that the enraged inferno instantly devoured anything in its path. Think I told myself, how many steps from the back door was my mother's grave; fifty steps, two hundred steps? Why can't I remember I fretted, mom's grave was supposed to be the easy one to find, but where is it? One of the men from the rescue team walked around the entire area moving some of the soot and debris around with a rake. "Don't worry we will find it," he commented. "We always do."

I was seriously concentrating on the man moving the ashes around, when one of the other rescue workers shouted from over near the burned cabin. "Hey, come look at this," he said. "The cement walls of this vault have protected the things stored underneath it. The roof laid on top of the two fallen walls and they all three worked as an insulator to shelter the items inside the cement vault from the intense fire." Then the man slowly got down on his hands and knees peering inside. Still looking inside the vault he asked me, "Was there anything in the vault besides food?"

My thoughts began to spin. "Yes, yes there were a lot of things. We had used it as a storage shed. That's where we had stored things to keep them dry and out of the way," I stuttered in disbelief.

The man that had been moving ashes around hollered for me to come see what he had found. "I think I may have found your mother's grave," he said. "Does this look familiar at all?" He questioned as he was digging up the end of a white bed sheet.

"Yes, that was what I wrapped my mother in to bury her," I said turning my head away to hold back the tears.

"You know Will, it would probably be better if you stand over by your grandpa for now, you don't have to be involved in this part of the rescue," he politely told me. "We can take it from here."

I felt very unsteady as I slowly walked over by my grandpa who was busy watching the helicopter crew look for my father. "They found Mom," I softly told him. Grandpa glanced back over towards my mom's remains; then he put his arm around my shoulder and kept us focused towards the helicopter workers.

The crew had been digging for hours with no sign of the bright orange Hummer. So, they decided to stop for lunch. It was odd eating lunch on the burned out, deserted, mountainside. It wasn't really a good picnic area, but that is where their work sight was, so that is where we ate.

After lunch, the man who had discovered the things in the cement storage vault requested the use of the helicopter for a few minutes. He wanted the pilot to move the cement walls away from the building, because the walls were too heavy for the men to move by themselves. Within seconds the huge helicopter had pulled away the heavy cement roof and walls that had folded over the vault to protect the contents that were stored inside.

As the helicopter crew returned to their work down in the canyon; Grandpa and I sorted through the salvaged remains of the cabin. Every single thing that was not in the vault was melted and burned until it was unrecognizable. Chairs, furniture, beds, everything was gone. We sifted through some melted plastic containers that had held dried food in the cement vault, and moved around several vegetable cans that had exploded from getting too hot.

Then I found the fire proof metal container that I had carefully stored some of our valuables in many months ago. It remained solid and intact and was barely touched or bent. I was sure that even being fire proof it wouldn't have withstood the intense heat of the forest fire without the protection of the cement wall covering. We cautiously dragged the metal container out into the yard area and began sorting through it. Inside the container we found Mom's jewelry box, our baby books, the wedding album, the family Bible and Mom's journal with the last letter that she had written to Clay and I. Inside each baby book was our birth certificate and passport. There were also, several other miscellaneous items that I had folded and put in the bottom of the metal chest. I looked up at Grandpa in total shock and said, "Grandpa I can't believe this. The entire forest was thoroughly destroyed, but our documents survived the fire, how can that be?"

Grandpa smiled at me with huge tears streaming down his face and just shrugged his shoulders.

As we sat there reminiscing and looking through some of the pictures, I told him, "Dad had haphazardly thrown everything into the back of the Hummer the night he brought us up to the mountain." I shook my head back and forth while sorting through everything in my lap, "That's how all of this stuff got up here at the cabin in the first place."

I thought back to that night and said, "You know Dad wasn't really thinking straight the night he drove us up here, he was really distraught, and so he just grabbed things and threw them in the back of the Hummer to bring with us."

Grandpa didn't question me he just nodded his head up and down, as if everything that had happened was the way it was supposed to be.

Before we could dwell too long on how the articles had survived the fire, the men working with the helicopter signaled they had found something buried under the huge masses of dirt and rocks. They had used some sort of enormous metal detector that could measure through tremendous debris; it was a large instrument that was used to find deeply buried items. It could detect metal from several feet inside the earth. The men had told us that if they got close enough to the vicinity of where the vehicle had been buried, they were sure their equipment could find it. And it did.

They dug away a lot of the area by hand, until they finally found a piece of the Hummer to hook onto with the helicopter. The crew had been working all day and it would soon be dark, so they decided to collect everything that we wanted to take back to Boise with us and then the crew could return tomorrow to finish uncovering the Hummer and my father's remains.

There would be no reason for my Grandfather and I to return to the mountain again, because the crew had discovered where the body was located and they didn't need our help any longer. They could collect his remains the following day and have them sent back to Boise for the coroner's office.

We loaded the metal boxes that contained my family's valuables into the big helicopter and two men loaded my mother's remains into the back compartment, so we were ready to head home.

I felt a deep emptiness in the pit of my stomach as I said my last goodbye to our cherished family mountain. This time I was sure I would never see my mother's Moon Mountain again; the place where the full moon shone the brightest, the place where you felt you could just reach out and touch the moon. It was the site where on one special anniversary the love of her life gave her everything, even the moon. It was once the most wonderful place on earth.

I sat quietly in the helicopter, all the way home, thinking confusing thoughts about our family's mountain. The fear and the hatred I had for

Moon Mountain had vanished. I knew the mountain could no longer hurt us. After returning to the mountain that day, I resolved that it was now just an ordinary mountain, a mountain that had been destroyed by a forest fire.

Grandpa and I were tired and hungry as we returned to Gowen Field that evening. As soon as we landed Grandpa called my grandma to tell her we were on our way home. She had fried chicken ready for dinner so we anxiously headed towards Eagle. We both loved Grandma's fried chicken so we could hardly wait to get home.

As we pulled into the driveway we saw Clayton waiting to open the gate for us, the off-duty policeman stood close behind him. Grandma had invited the private policeman to stay for dinner too. Apparently, their day had been uneventful, but Grandpa was glad he had hired someone to stay with them for the day.

I was starved. She had made fried chicken, real mashed potatoes, homemade biscuits and gravy, fresh warm applesauce, corn-on-the-cob, and homemade berry cobbler with ice cream for desert. I had seconds on everything. Dinner was so delicious, I felt like I had died and gone to heaven.

The policeman stayed and visited for a few minutes while he drank his coffee after dinner. Grandpa paid him for the day and let him know we would not be going back up on the mountain the next day. He told him, "The crew found both of the bodies and we brought our daughter-in-law's body back today, and they will be bringing our son's remains back to Boise tomorrow."

I sat across the room and listened as Grandpa talked to the man. I glanced over at Clayton and watched his expression as they talked so openly about our dead parent's remains. Poor Clayton, he looked so pale sitting in his chair listening to everyone talk. Clayton was not even fourteen years old yet and he shouldn't have to listen to all this talk of death and dead bodies. My incredibly handsome little brother, what goes on in your head, I ask myself as I watched him from across the room. So often in the past two years you have just listened and accepted. What a remarkable person my parents created when they had Clayton.

As I sat there watching the anguish in my younger brother's face, I closed my eyes and prayed for him, "May the rest of your life be full of blessings, my admirable baby brother." I opened my eyes to see the policeman saying goodnight to my grandparents. He reminded them to call him if they needed him again.

Clayton and I went into the family room to watch some football while Grandpa brought Grandma Suzanne up to date on everything that had happened that day. Around 10:30 we headed for bed, it had been a long few days. I slept like a log, because I was finally at peace with the mountain.

THIRTEEN

The next morning the two detectives came by to let us know what they had discovered about the bloody sign. "We found the man who worked for your father; his wife died about fourteen months ago," the first detective said. "His bloody fingerprints on the sign, matched up with the fingerprints that were taken at your father's company. Apparently the company had a security policy of doing fingerprint and background checks on all of their employees every single year, so finding him and matching him up with the sign, was relatively easy. The man's name was Henry Balconer; does that name mean anything to any of you?"

We all shook our heads and said no.

"Well, he was a night security guard at your father's company for over twenty years. In fact he had worked there for several years before your father even took over as the CEO. We also discovered when we went to his house that he only lived a little over a mile from here. We checked with his neighbors, and they told us that he had been very depressed after he lost his job. His wife had been sick for several months before the company even closed, and they had spent every bit of their savings for her hospital stays and surgeries. When the company went down and he lost his job, he was desperate because he had no more insurance or income for her treatments." Looking down at his notes he solemnly said, "His wife died within four months of him losing his job."

"Oh that poor man, that's terrible!" my grandma exclaimed. "What can we do to help him?" Can we go see him face to face and maybe help him financially to get back on his feet?" she suggested.

"Well, actually," the second detective spoke up as he cleared his throat, and oddly looked over at the first detective. "Mrs. Richardson that won't be necessary the man was not well himself, he was a hemophiliac." The officer stammered on, "We believe that when he cut himself to write the threatening sign to you that he bled to death before he could even get back home and into his house. The officer shook his head and said, "We found him lying dead at his back doorway, he was half inside and half outside of his old neglected house." The officer went on, "The coroner's report stated that his time of death was essentially two days before your family got back from Florida. He must have left the sign on the fence earlier than we thought, not the day you returned." The detective said, "Apparently he was already dead by the time you even found the sign."

"That poor guy," my grandpa Bill said. "He must have been angry with Clinton all of this time, and he didn't even know that Clinton was already gone. Well, thank you so much gentlemen," Grandpa told the men as he shook each man's hand. "At least now we have some answers."

Grandma Suzanne then stood up and always being the gracious host said, "I have fresh coffee and warm cinnamon rolls that I just took out of the oven, if it wouldn't be too improper to offer you some refreshments before you leave?"

The two men smiled at each other and said, "actually ma'am neither one of us are even working until later on today. We just wanted to come by together to tell you what we had found so your family wouldn't have to worry any longer."

Grandpa Bill smiled and said, "Well gentlemen, we'll take that as a yes to the coffee and cinnamon rolls then. Let's go sit down at the kitchen table. We're a little short on furniture; it hasn't arrived here from Florida yet."

My grandparents loved having company, just like my parents did. It felt so good to have life going through our house again.

As the men sat and enjoyed their coffee in the kitchen, the front doorbell rang. When I answered it, I discovered it was the policeman that had been there the day before. Apparently, he had forgotten a baseball cap that he had been wearing, and he left it out on the deck. When he went to find it, he saw his two friends sitting in the kitchen drinking coffee with my grandpa.

Of course Grandma Suzanne motioned for him to come in and sit down and she instantly fixed him a gooey cinnamon roll and poured him some fresh coffee too. Grandpa Bill and the three men sat in the kitchen and discussed all of the events of the past several days. They talked like they had been good friends for years. It was great to sit back and quietly listen to them talk. Grandma was right, we are a good family. The policeman stayed and visited for a couple of hours.

Later on that afternoon, we got a call from the coroner's office, and the rescue team had uncovered my father's remains and they had safely brought him down from the mountain. We were told that both of my parent's bodies were being evaluated and could soon be processed for funeral services.

After hearing the news I watched Clayton get out of his chair and calmly walk into his bedroom and close the door. I figured he just needed some time to himself for awhile.

Suddenly, my thoughts were gripped with fear as I remembered the day my father first went over the mountain. I leaped out of my chair and ran down the hall shouting at the top of my lungs, "Clayton, Clayton, Clayton I screamed, no Clay not again."

I barged into his bedroom screaming like a mad man. I flung open his door, and saw Clayton sitting soberly at his desk. "What are you doing in here?" I shouted praying he could reply.

"What do you mean, what am I doing in here?" he innocently said. "I'm writing two goodbye letters, one to Mom and one to Dad. I wanted to tell them how much I loved them, you know like the way Mom had written to us?" he said proudly. "What's the matter? Why were you screaming at me?"

"I just got scared for a minute," I said flustered, as my grandparents entered the room after racing down the hall behind me.

"Why are you screaming?" Grandma asked.

"Scared about what?" Grandpa Bill asked as he came into the room.

Clay looked up at me, and then he understood. "Oh Will, I'm sorry, I didn't even think about that. It's going to be all right, Mom and Dad have been dead for a long time," he said trying to comfort me.

"What are you boys talking about?" Grandpa Bill demanded. "William, why would you be scared because your brother went into his bedroom?"

I looked over at Clayton then back over to Grandpa, "Well, after Dad died Clayton had problems for awhile."

"Problems, what kind of problems? Grandma asked.

Clayton spoke up then, "It happened the day that Dad went over the side of the mountain. My mind went into shock or something and I was not able to talk for awhile." He looked right at me as he explained, "Will I am so sorry, when I came into my room I never thought about you fearing I would go into shock again."

"What do you mean? You went into shock and were unable to talk for awhile?" Grandpa questioned in his Doctor voice. "What else went on, up on that mountain that Grandma and I should know about?" Grandpa acted kind of angry, "Every time we turn around we learn something new that we haven't heard about before. How long were you unable to talk Clayton, one week, two weeks?"

Clayton looked at me and carefully chose his words before he looked back at Grandpa, "Over a year I guess," Clayton said hesitantly.

"A year! Grandpa shouted. "Clay are you all right now? Do you need to see a specialist?"

"No I don't think so Grandpa, I've been all right for a long time." Clay said respectfully. "Don't you think so, Will?"

"To be honest with you, I have never even thought about it again until just now, when he silently went into his room," I answered truthfully.

Grandma said, "Then we'll accept that, and we don't need to talk about that dreadful mountain again." Then she turned and walked out of the room with Grandpa behind her.

After they closed the door Clayton looked over at me and said, "I guess we shouldn't tell them about the wolves and the bears."

We both grinned at each other and I answered, "Probably not."

Early the following morning the shipping truck arrived from Florida with all of my grandparent's furniture. Grandma and Grandpa were busy all day unloading boxes and placing furniture in empty rooms and organizing the deck and pool area. We could tell that Grandma was thrilled to be able to use her own things again. They would help make our house, her house. In one day she had the house looking like she had been there forever. My mom would be pleased.

Grandpa also arranged some of his things in my dad's den. I found that a little difficult to accept, because it had always been my dad's area. I had to once again remind myself that my dad was never coming back, and he wouldn't need it anymore.

FOURTEEN

Later on that evening my grandfather received a phone call from George, one of the helicopter pilots who had rescued us from the mountain. I could hear my grandfather talking to the pilot, but I couldn't quite understand what was being said. "Yes, Well that is nice of you to call," my grandfather commented answering in a courteous tone. "I'm sure the boys would be glad to meet with you for dinner, but let me check with my wife to make sure we don't have something else planned tomorrow evening." As I stood there listening to my grandfather talk on the phone, I noticed him writing down the pilot's phone number, then he politely said goodbye and told him he would call him right back.

After he hung up the phone he motioned for me to follow him into the kitchen to find my grandmother and Clayton. I followed close behind because I was anxious to find out why one of the helicopter pilots would be calling our house.

We found Grandma and Clayton fixing dinner in the kitchen; and I figured out that Grandpa was waiting to discuss the phone call with all of us at the same time. When we were all together he said, "I just received a call from George, one of the helicopter pilots that had rescued you from Moon Mountain. The two pilots would like to take us all out to dinner tomorrow night at The Cottonwood Grill, in downtown Boise. They want to talk to both of you boys and to apologize to you in person." Grandpa hesitated before continuing, "Apparently, the two pilots are upset with themselves because they didn't pay enough attention to you when they found you up on the mountain, they didn't even ask you your last name. They didn't realize who you were until my lawyer, Mr. Jenkins contacted them last week to find out the area where they had rescued you. Mr. Jenkins knew that the pilots would have the location documented. We needed the exact location to find the cabin property, so that we could find your parent's bodies."

Grandpa continued talking, "The pilots had no idea that you had been trapped up on the mountain for two years. They thought you were drug addicts because you looked so filthy and unkempt." Grandpa hung his head then continued, "The pilot that called me said that they took you down to the fire camp and left you there because they were busy, and they didn't want to waste their time with you. They thought you were in trouble, and they didn't want to get involved."

"That's terrible," Grandma Suzanne gasped as she listened to my grandpa talk. "Our boys have never done anything wrong, yet they are continually questioned by everyone," She said shaking her head as she wiped her hands on a dishtowel.

Grandpa looked at Clay and I and said, "They want to take our family out to dinner to apologize for their misunderstanding. When the attorney called them and told them who you were, they felt terrible."

Grandpa put his face in his hands and then rubbed his hands over his hair before continuing on, "They said they couldn't believe that you were the Richardson boys that had disappeared along with your parents almost two years ago. The pilot told me that he and Dallas, the other helicopter pilot, had been part of the original search team that was sent out to look for you right after we reported you missing. He said that they had spent several days volunteering looking for your family." Grandpa shook his head and said, "The pilot told me that if they had only asked you your last name they would have known immediately who you were. They could not believe that after two years they had accidentally found you and didn't even know it, because that wasn't even the area they had initially been searching in." Grandpa looked at me with a concerned look on his face and concluded, "It's up to you boys, if you don't want to meet with them your grandmother and I will understand."

Up until now Clay and I had remained quiet, just listening to the strange events that Grandpa had been telling us. We both stood there in the kitchen trying to decide what we should do. I knew that I wasn't angry with the pilots for dropping us off at the fire camp, but I wasn't sure how my little brother felt.

Then Clayton spoke up and I realized that he wasn't angry either, because he said, "Well, they did save our lives, so I guess it couldn't hurt to go and meet them for dinner."

I slowly shook my head up and down in agreement and said, "It might be nice to see our rescuers in better circumstances." So, Grandpa called the pilot back to tell him we would accept their dinner invitation.

The following evening we went out to have dinner with our heroes, the pilots from the fire camp. I was worried about seeing someone that we knew at the restaurant, and we still hadn't talked to anyone since we got home. Luckily the restaurant was dark and our table was in a far corner so we didn't see many people.

We visited with Dallas and George and their wives, Julie and Jill for over two hours. It turned out to be a really great evening. The pilots were both very easy to talk with and even their wives asked us questions about our confinement on Moon Mountain. They couldn't believe that we had been trapped up on the mountain for so long, and that we had survived through so much.

Dallas said, "We searched for your family for several weeks after you first disappeared. No one could believe that you had just vanished without any tangible leads."

George said, "Many of the volunteers in the search parties had refused to give up searching, because they were personal friends of your family. That is what upsets me the worst. After two years we finally found you, and then we just left you at the fire camp and flew away without even asking you any questions."

I told Dallas and George repeatedly, "We are just thankful you were there at the right time and could get us down from the mountain. We will always be grateful to both of you for saving our lives."

I could not count how many times Dallas and George apologized to us that night, so I'm glad we went out to dinner with them. They were really nice people and Clayton and I owed them so much. It seemed like every day the lost pieces of our lives were slowly going back together.

FIFTEEN

After going out to dinner with the two pilots, Grandpa decided it was time to do a press release and tell everyone about our family. The pilots were the only people that we had actually talked to since our return, so it was time to let everyone know that we were back. We had safely gotten my mom and my dad down from the mountain, and Grandpa wanted to let people know that both of my parents were deceased. This was also his way of announcing to the community that Clayton and I were still alive and we were back home living in Eagle. I don't know what he wrote, I didn't want to read it, but my grandfather was a very intelligent man and I'm sure he was very straightforward, honest and diplomatic.

A press release was probably the best way for everything to be handled. It would save Clayton and I a lot of time of trying to explain everything to everyone over and over again. I did not feel like telling people how horrible my world had been since we left home that dreadful night two years ago, but I knew our story somehow had to be told.

The press release had gone out the day before, and I was feeling very apprehensive, I felt like a time bomb, slowly ticking away ready to explode. I was sure that by now, most of my family's old friends had received the news of our return, but we hadn't heard from anyone. I paced around outside in the yard for awhile trying to figure out what I needed to do. I was afraid to talk to anybody, but I was even more afraid, not talking to anyone. I had no idea what people would think about us. Would they hate my father for hiding us away? Would they think something was wrong with my brother and I after being isolated for so long? Will people even remember us?

I decided to head for my room and try to calm my nerves. I plopped down on the top of my bedspread and stared up at the ceiling. As I lay there looking up at my ceiling light, I realized that I had overwhelming fears of my future. I had so many questions about my friends, and about my parent's funeral, and what people would be saying about our family. My mind wouldn't slow down. As I lay there on my Bronco bedspread, in my comfortable private bedroom, I should have felt happy and contented because I was home and I was safe and secure, but I didn't.

I kept thinking about how deeply children depend on their parents. I don't think that most kids even stop to think about how much courage they have, because of the support of their father and mother. Teenagers are a lot braver when they have a dad and mom who are always there for them. Until my family was destroyed I never thought about it either. Your mom and dad guard your back. Your family is your army. They are your strength, they are your identity, and they are always there to hold you up.

When I was young and I would worry about certain things, I would go home from school and talk to my mom, and within a few minutes I would feel better without even telling her I was upset about anything. Moms just make you feel O.K. Your dad and mom rejoice when times are good and they are sad when you are sad. Your parents scream the loudest when you make that final touchdown. Your mom is the one who takes the pictures of the crazy events of your life; then she stores them away in an album so that one day you can show them to your children and your grandchildren. "Who will be my children's grandparents?" I unexpectedly thought as more confusing questions scrambled through my head.

Although, my phone was working, I had never turned it on. I had so much uncertainty and I couldn't get myself to face it. I lay quietly in my room, looking at the wrinkled picture of Hailie and my mom and I wished once again that things could have been different. Then I tucked the picture back into my wallet.

As I lay there looking up at my ceiling, I could hear car horns honking off in the distance. "What is going on?" I thought. The honking seemed louder, as I abruptly walked out of my bedroom and on down the hall.

I noticed my grandparents and my brother were already headed out of the door by the time I reached the front of the house. I walked out into the driveway and stood beside them as car after car streamed in through our gates and down our lane. I looked over at my disbelieving grandparents and they both shrugged their shoulders, and then I looked at my brother who appeared to be just as surprised as I was.

We saw cars full of people, with their lights on and horns honking coming from miles and miles up the road. An old cream colored Volvo with a solid black painted hood led the precession straight to our doorstep. Before the Volvo even came to a complete stop, the passenger-side door opened and out jumped a tall slender teenage girl with shoulder-length bouncy dark hair. The young girl came running across the yard and literally leaped into my arms, hugging me and sobbing into my shoulder. "Oh Will, I can't believe it's you," Hailie cried as she hugged me so tight I could hardly breathe. "Do you know how long I have prayed for you to come back home?" She uttered into my ear as she wept into my neck. We must have been quite a sight standing there grasping on to each other, not wanting to ever let go.

I am positive that the rest of the world came to a complete stop that afternoon, as I stood there in front of hundreds of people holding my beautiful, Hailie Loo securely in my arms. It felt like I was dreaming as I inhaled the clean, fresh scent of her shampoo as her soft thick hair brushed against my face. I had known her since we were in the first grade, but that was the closest I had ever been to her. We were both barely fourteen when I had disappeared. At fourteen our parents had allowed us to be boyfriend and girlfriend, but they said we were too young to go out on dates. So, I had never even hugged her before that.

Nothing seemed true, I felt like I was having an amazing illusion, everything was moving in slow motion, everything seemed perfect, so I knew it couldn't really be happening, but it was.

It took me a few seconds to come to my senses and then I finally became aware that car doors were slamming up and down the driveway and road. I slowly released Hailie and stood her beside me. It was then that I noticed all of the television cameras and vans from several local television stations. They had arrived with the rest of the procession of vehicles. Wherever I looked I saw flashes coming from the cameras of newspaper and magazine photographers. There were people taking pictures everywhere. Apparently our family had become big news since the story of my parent's deaths had been released. It was crazy, there were people everyplace. I could see people walking from clear down the street. They had parked their cars on the road and started walking towards our property. It was like a carnival with crowds of spectators coming from every edge of the county. I found it hard to breathe with so many people around me. Clayton and I had spent so much time alone, that it was difficult to have all of the hordes of people surrounding us and hanging on our every word.

I put a fake smile on my face and continued to greet people and I tried really hard to act pleased to see them. They were all so nice to my brother and I and I had to keep reminding myself that they were only there because of us.

Grandpa had opened the gate to the field so that people could park out in the mowed pasture. He was just as surprised to see all of these people as we were, but he could tell he needed to create a parking lot in a hurry. People had come from everywhere. They were carrying food, tables, chairs, gifts, and pop. I saw people surrounding us from every direction smiling and crying at the same time.

I recognized people from church, from our school and from my dad's work; and out of the cream colored Volvo with the black painted hood came Michael, Shauna, Duke, Tyson and Devon. My brain was on overload, everything seemed foggy, but it was real. My friends, my friends were really here, but they all seemed so much older than I remembered. Michael was tall and thin and he had shoulder-length straight brown hair with blond highlights from the summer sun. When we bear-hugged I could tell that we were both about the same height. He was holding on tightly to Shauna's hand, so I could see things hadn't changed much there.

Next I saw my friend Darrek Harriss, we all called him Duke, and he too had long hair only his was more of a light-brown color. A pretty dark-haired girl that I didn't recognize walked up and stood beside him. Duke looked over at her and smiled and I figured she must have been his girlfriend.

I kept walking around in a haze. It was like everything was moving in an unhurried rhythm. Nothing seemed genuine. My mind was not prepared for seeing all of these people at once.

Behind Duke and Devon came their parents, Darren and Sammy Harriss. They brought Mrs. Harriss' famous chocolate chip cookies and handed the plate to me. I instantly took a bite of her melt-in-your mouth chocolate morsels and I was in heaven. I grabbed a napkin to wipe the chocolate off of my face, and then I hid the entire plate up on the deck so that no one else could find it. I planned to eat the delicious cookies she had made for me later, after everyone was gone.

Hailie stood back as I hugged Kennedy, Ron, Ashlynn and Abby.

Kennedy, my mom's best friend held me tight for several seconds as she tearfully told me how sorry she was for all that we had been through. I just nodded my head up and down. I had nothing to say.

People started putting food out on the picnic tables and Grandma and Grandpa brought out paper plates and silverware. There were people all over, and everyplace I looked I saw familiar faces. Faces I had only dreamed about ever seeing again.

Then I noticed Clay standing across the yard a few feet from me talking to Devon, and he looked about as out of place as I did. Everyone was so kind and thoughtful, but the entire world just seemed completely overwhelming. So much had gone on in the past few months and it was hard for our minds to digest everything.

Hailie wouldn't leave my side. She quietly just stood about two feet away from me, watching my every move. I guess she thought I might disappear again. She was so gorgeous, I was almost afraid to look at her. It was odd, because I had never been embarrassed around her before, but she had grown into such a beautiful, graceful young lady. I was intimidated. She was no longer the little innocent looking, longhaired, freckled faced Hailie Loo that was in the picture that I carried in my wallet. Her hair was dark-brown, about shoulder-length, and it was full and bouncy. She wore light make-up to accent her magnificent baby-blue eyes, and she was poised and feminine and attractive beyond belief. She was incredible; I wished my mom was there to see her.

Hailie had finally stopped crying and instead, she was smiling and laughing as she talked to everyone. Every time I'd glance over her way, she would smile that smile at me that would take my breath away. I hoped I was smiling back at her, because when she smiled at me I'd totally lose my senses and my mind would go all fuzzy and I couldn't even think straight.

It wasn't until later on that evening that I noticed my friend Tyson was being extra quiet, he had hardly even talked to me. He stood back out of the way, kind of over by Hailie. Then I realized something was going on, because the next time that I looked at Hailie I noticed Tyson had her facing towards him, keeping her back towards me. He seemed to be having a very serious conversation with her. My heart stopped beating, as I watched as Tyson put his arm around her shoulder and they walked off together, never even looking back at me.

I wanted to run away and hide. "Of course Hailie would have another boyfriend," I thought. "What was I thinking?" I had been gone for two years and she wouldn't stop living just because I disappeared. She was only fourteen years old when I left, and she was charming, smiley, captivating and amazing, she always has been. I just wanted to run and get away from all of these people, but I knew I couldn't do that because they were all here to encourage me. So, even if I felt like dying inside, I did what I had learned to do over and over again in the past two years; just act like nothing was wrong.

I saw Michael's parent's Mr. and Mrs. Jeffreys, standing across the yard talking to Coach Pease and his wife. Michael's grandparent's Gene and Jackie Jeffreys were standing there too. They were such nice people. We had all gone to church together before our family disappeared. Michael's mother, Debi, looked over at me and smiled, and when I smiled back at her she came over and hugged me and she started to cry. Mrs. Jeffreys had always been so nice to me. I had known her since

Michael and I started kindergarten. Debi was my mother's first friend in Idaho.

Mr. and Mrs. Ryan were standing across the yard talking to Hailie's parents and Mr. Hammond, the vice-principal and his wife, Julie. When I looked over their way, all six of them started walking towards me to share their condolences about the death of my parents.

Mr. Ryan gave me a strong bear hug and held onto me for several seconds before he patted me on the back and told me how pleased he was to have Clayton and I back home safely. He told me that we could return to school the following week if we wanted to. He said we could get some tutoring until we got back up to our grade level. He was confidant that from our past test scores that we could easily bring our grades back up to the level of the rest of our classmates. He felt the state would credit the past two years as some sort of home schooling if we could bring all of our current classes up-to-date. Mr. Ryan then shook my hand and said, "William, we will all be so glad to have you and Clayton back in school."

Hailie's mom and dad stood there with tears in their eyes, trying to tell me how pleased they were to have us back home, but Hailie's mom seemed more distraught than most of the people were. She could barely even talk, she was so disturbed. She finally just excused herself and walked over to stand by some other people that we had gone to church with.

I noticed a large group of people standing over on the far side of the yard, and they were standing off by themselves. I recognized Mr. Dee, my father's overseas representative standing with Mrs. Henning, Dad's secretary, and Kathy and Mickey from the reception desk, but they were the only ones that I knew. The rest of people must have been people from my father's work, but I didn't know any of them.

When Mrs. Henning saw me watching her she came over to pay her respects, but she couldn't stop crying as she talked to Clay and I. She had sincerely loved our family and she couldn't bear hearing all of the problems our family had been through. She told me she hadn't worked since the day that the plant had closed. She asked us to stop by her house in a few days, then she said, "I have something that had belonged to your father and I need to give it to you."

"Probably some M&M's," I thought to myself. Grandpa wrote down her address and said we would go by in a day or so.

Greyson James, my dad's golfing buddy was at a loss for words when he talked to me. "Your dad was a great guy, always remember that," was all that he could say as he gave me a hug, and instantly turned his head away. He and my dad had been the best of friends. We used to all three play golf together every Saturday as I was growing up.

One of the ladies from our church, Mrs. Smith, invited Grandma to come to the ladies Bible Study with her. Grandma was delighted to have a new friend. Our family had known Gertrude and Willis Smith ever since we came to Idaho. They were wonderful people and they appeared to be around the same age as my grandparents. I was sure Grandma Suzanne and Gertrude would become great friends. My grandma never complained about moving to Idaho, but I'm sure she missed her old friends back in Florida.

By the time people started to leave, I think I had hugged everyone that I had known in my lifetime, and every one of them seemed happy to have us back in town again.

Finally Michael, Shauna, Duke, Tyson and Hailie came over to say goodbye. The goodbye was a lot calmer than when we had first said hello. I gave Michael, Duke and Tyson, a macho handshake, and told them I would see them at school on Monday. Then I hugged Shauna goodbye and I couldn't even look Hailie in the face. I looked towards the ground and gently put my arms around her waist to give her a short goodbye hug, like I had Shauna; but before I could let her go she quickly wrapped her arms around my neck and kissed me on the cheek. She whispered so that only I could hear, "Will Richardson, I have missed you more than you can ever imagine." Then she slipped out of my arms and wiped the tears from her eyes as she hurried and got into Michael's car.

I just stood there stunned, as I watched the cream colored Volvo disappear down Eagle Road. I let out a huge sigh as I continued to stand there feeling more mixed up than I had earlier. Grandpa closed the pasture gate as Grandma and Clay straightened up the deck area. Our visitors had put most everything back in order before they left, so there really wasn't much to clean up. We had several bags of trash to send with the trash pick up on Tuesday, but everything else looked pretty good.

"The kids look great," Grandpa Bill said to me as he was picking up a paper napkin off of the ground.

"Yes they do" I laughingly answered. "But they seem so much older than they did when I left." I pondered my thoughts for a minute, "Did you see Michael's car? It used to be his mother's car and his parents gave it to him after they bought a new one." I kept talking, "He said it runs great, but he had a small rear end collision a few months after he first got his driver's license. The person in front of him stopped quickly and he bumped into him. That's why the hood is black."

"We need to think about you getting your driver's license Will," Grandpa said. "I think we'll sign you up for private lessons next week, so you can get it sooner if that's all right with you."

"Next week?" I exclaimed. "That would be great."

Grandma Suzanne came out on the deck just then, and she looked around and said, "Wasn't that wonderful of all of those people to come over to the house like that?" Grandma kept talking like she was puzzled, "Did you know that Duke's mother, Sammy, and Mr. Ryan along with many of the teachers started an e-mail and phone chain after they received the press release yesterday? They contacted each family from the school and the church and they organized everyone to meet in the church parking lot so that people could come out as a caravan. Gertrude Smith told me that," Grandma bragged. "She also told me that Sammy Harriss got a hold of Mrs. Henning so that she could contact all of your father's old employees. Isn't that incredible? That's why there were so many people here."

I glanced over at my grandmother and grinned, she was so much like my mom, the more the merrier was always my mom's attitude too.

"It just shows you boys how much your family was truly loved," Grandma said while wiping the tears from her face. "I bet you boys were glad to see all of your friends again?" Grandma looked down at her hands and uttered, "Grandpa and I got to know most of the kids really well after you disappeared." Grandma then looked over at me and said, "Hailie has sure grown into a beautiful young lady, and she is such a nice girl. She sure seems glad to have you back William. Didn't she used to be your girlfriend?"

I nodded my head up and down and walked over to the deck and grabbed the cookies I had hidden that Mrs. Harriss had made for me. I quickly looked around and I saw that everything was straightened up so I decided to head for my room. "Goodnight," I hollered as I walked into the house. I really didn't feel like talking anymore.

"Goodnight" Clayton and my grandparents responded back to me almost at the same time.

I walked into my room and flung myself down on my bed. Then I reached into my back pocket and pulled out my wallet with the picture of Hailie with my mom. My Hailie Loo...that wasn't her real name of course, that was just the nickname her grandma and I had called her. Her real name was Hailie Nicole. Then I let out a discouraged sigh and said to myself, "That picture was taken another lifetime ago."

Again I knew without a doubt that every one in the world had gone on without me, and I wasn't sure if I would ever be able to fit in again. I lay the picture of Mom and Hailie down on the nightstand, and then I reached for a couple of Mrs. Harriss' yummy cookies. "Cookies always make a person feel better," I said to myself. "And I get to start driver's training next week," I randomly thought, as I closed my eyes for a second. I was totally exhausted from talking to so many people, and then I accidentally fell asleep on top of the covers.

I dreamed about driving my little Mini Cooper down Eagle Road. It was the same dream that I had dreamed night after night, for the first few months after I got my car. People up and down Eagle Road would smile and wave to me as I drove by in my perfect little yellow mini. My dad would say to me, "This engine is so quiet, it just purrs. I am so glad your mother and I chose this little mini for you Will. We couldn't decide on red or yellow, but your mom thought you would like the yellow one the best. And of course she was right, and we could hardly wait to give it to you." Dad would say, "You really are a great driver Will." Then he would beam from ear to ear, as I drove my awesome little Mini Cooper down the street. He was so proud me.

I was so excited about my new car, my entire life was perfect, but when I looked over to see my dad; my body froze like ice and I sat straight up in my bed. My dad is dead, I instantly remembered. He is at the morgue getting ready for his funeral. Then I felt sick all over because I was awake enough by then to remember my Mini Cooper was gone too. I reached around behind me and grabbed my pillow and buried my face in it to keep from screaming out loud. I hadn't dreamed that dream for a long time. What made me dream it that night?

My Dad had chosen that mini just for me. It even had special blue and orange pinstriped Boise State flames on the front fenders, coming out from the headlights and around the front wheels. Dad had someone put the shaded flames on it before he gave it to me, because he wanted to make my car unique and he knew I loved Boise State so much. That's why my mom chose yellow instead of red, and that's what made it the coolest car there ever was. I loved the flames and I loved my dad and mom because they had picked that certain car out for me. My grandparents had even got me a personalized license plate that said, "WLLSWLS" which of course stood for Will's Wheels.

I was shaking all over. "I hadn't dreamed that dream since my dad died," I thought to myself. "It must have been because my grandpa had told me I could take drivers training next week."

I got out of bed and involuntarily walked down the hall to the kitchen and got some cold milk out of the fridge. I knew that Grandma always kept slices of cheese in the refrigerator, so I sat down and slowly nibbled on some cheese and started thinking of all of the things that had gone on in the past few days. So many changes and so many faces floating around inside my head, I thought of Michael, Duke, Shauna, Tyson and Hailie.

"Tyson is a great guy," I thought. "He was always so talented and smart. Of course Tyson is whom she would choose. Actually they are really a good-looking couple. Very well matched I tried to convince myself. Tyson is fairly tall, dark and handsome. Hailie is graceful, intelligent, confident and funny, and her cute little freckles darting across her nose always intrigued me. She is stylish, easy to talk to, honest, and her smile, that melt your heart smile of hers." I sighed as I ran my hands over my hair and thought to myself, "She is such a classy person and she is so drop-dead gorgeous, and...She used to be my girlfriend and my best friend." I shook my head back and forth trying to clear my head, and then I lectured myself again, "But I was forced to be gone for two years, so of course she went on with her life."

"Well, at least I get to start driver's training next week," I said to myself trying to cheer myself up as I turned the lights off and headed on down the hall to my bedroom. I entered my room and realized Clay wasn't there, apparently he had stayed in his own room all night. I got ready for bed, and then I picked up the picture of Hailie and my beloved mother from the nightstand. I stared at the old picture for several seconds before slipping it back into its special hiding place in my wallet. I feared going back to sleep, I was afraid I would dream about my dad and my car again, but I didn't when I closed my eyes all I could see was Hailie.

Early the next morning Clay came running down the hall with the newspaper in his hand and shouted, "Hey, lazy bones wake up so you can see yourself on the front page of The Idaho Statesman."

I stared in disbelief, because there covering almost the entire front page was my beautiful Hailie with her arms wrapped tightly around my neck and my face clearly buried in her gorgeous soft hair. There were three whole pages of pictures and articles talking about our family and the hundreds of people who had come by to welcome us back home. Unlike the stories that appeared in the newspaper after our disappearance, the complete article was upbeat, flattering, and complimentary. After Clay left the room I tore off the section of Hailie and I and hung it inside my closet door where no one would find it.

SIXTEEN

Monday morning I was scared to death to go back to school. As often as I had dreamed about my school while I was up on Moon Mountain, I was now truly terrified to go into my classes. I felt like I did when I was five years old and going to kindergarten for the very first time.

I went into the office and was given the list of rooms I needed to go to throughout the day. Then I took a deep breath and slowly opened the door to my first class period. I felt so out of place. I was afraid to look up at anyone, and then out of the corner of my eye I saw Michael's hand waving to me to sit over by him. It was just like when we were five years old. Michael, my good buddy Michael; he was my mentor when I was five, and he was my mentor again at sixteen.

After each class time ended the rest of the kids laughed and hollered as they walked up and down the halls, but I kept fairly quiet. I hadn't talked to anyone but Clay for the past two years, so it was hard for me talk to people. I think every student at the school had seen my picture on the front page of the newspaper. Because every guy that walked by me slugged me on the shoulder and acted like I had never even been gone. That picture was a good icebreaker for me it helped me to be able to talk a little easier to every one that I saw.

Finally a girl named Shayla that I had known since grade school, came up and stood by me and asked, "How is your first day back at school?" Before I could answer she leaned over and whispered in my ear, "You look a little lost." She must have been able to tell I was struggling to get back into the group.

I sighed as I confided in her, "I have thought about being back at school everyday for two years, but now that I am back I feel like I can't even carry on a conversation with anyone. I have been gone for so long that I don't even know what to say most of the time."

It wasn't until then that I looked directly into her face and I realized how beautiful Shayla had become. She had perfect, straight, white teeth and flawless olive skin, with shoulder-length light blond hair and dark brown eyes. I had known her for a long time and we had always been really good friends, but she was a lot prettier now than I had remembered. Shayla was easy to talk to and she was one of Hailie's best girlfriends. She had such a unique way about her; she looked directly into your eyes when you were talking to her like she was really interested in what you were talking about. She was the kind of person that made you feel welcome. She soon had me laughing and feeling more at ease.

At lunchtime a bunch of us sat together around the tables outside. We had Michael, Shauna, Shayla, Duke and his cute dark-haired girlfriend, Juliana, and of course Hailie and Tyson. I sat down across from Michael and Shayla came over and sat beside me. Every one of them could hardly wait to tell me what had been going on for the past several months. I hadn't been keeping track of time, so I had no idea even what date it was, but it was great listening to them all talk at once. We laughed and joked and for the first time in months I felt like an ordinary teenager.

Hailie and Tyson were both really quiet, but I tried not to notice because I was enjoying all of the innocent laughter and the stories they were telling me. I hadn't laughed that much since before I disappeared. It felt great!

When I got home that night Grandpa had made arrangements for me to start driver's training just as he had promised. I had lots of homework plus my new private driver's training classes, so my life was going to be really busy for awhile, and I loved it.

At dinner that night Clayton talked continuously about everything he and Devon had done at school that day. He was beaming and laughing and explaining everything that each person had said to him throughout his classes. He was so glad to be back at school. He too seemed more normal.

After dinner was over, and Clay and I had finished sharing about our day at school, Grandma and Grandpa told us we needed to help make arrangements for our parent's funerals. I knew that I would be kind of relieved once their funeral services were over with. Nothing could be as bad as the past several months had been. We decided on a simple service on Friday afternoon. It was determined that my parents would be buried at Cloverdale Cemetery out on Fairview and Cloverdale. Grandpa said he would make all of the final arrangements while we were at school the next day. I knew that the whole funeral process had to be very difficult for my grandparents, because they were not only burying their son; they were also burying their beautiful loving daughter-in-law.

My mother's sister, Margaret, flew in from Baltimore. Clayton and I hadn't seen her since we were little. Aunt Margaret was poised, quiet and slender and looked just like our mother. When we picked her and her husband Tom up at the Boise Airport I stared at her in disbelief. I would have sworn it was my mother walking through the air terminal doors. It was like God had given Clay and I one last glance of our mother healthy and beautiful again, walking in the body of our Aunt Margaret. We were so glad they had come for the funeral. The first night they got there, the six of us stayed up until 1:00 in the morning visiting about everything we could think of. It was wonderful hearing the stories of my mother's childhood.

The funeral wasn't as easy to get through as I had first thought it would be. I think every single person that my parents had known, came to pay their respects at their funeral service. It was the largest funeral the funeral parlor had ever had. There were people standing outside because it was too crowded for them to get into the building.

Mr. Ryan had excused any of the students and teachers from our school that wished to attend the funeral, so Clayton and I had many of our friends there, along with their parents and most of the teachers. My grandparents were very pleased with the outpouring of love and generosity by our school, the church and the community.

Clayton and I had gone from being totally alone for two years, to having hundreds of people hugging us and giving us their condolences. We were both completely dazed by all of the people that attended the funeral. When it was finally over and we again said our closing good-byes to our loving parents, we were both beyond exhausted.

I have to admit, my grandma and grandpa were right though, it was nice having my parent's buried together in a cemetery in town. It was a safe place where we could always go and see them. It gave us a sense of peace and closure just to know everything was finally settled.

Our aunt and uncle stayed for two extra days then they were off to Baltimore again. They promised to keep in touch this time and we made plans to go visit them the following summer. Grandma took down all the information that we needed and we looked forward to meeting our cousins for the very first time. Saying goodbye to Aunt Margaret at the airport that day was a little unsettling because it was like saying goodbye to our beautiful mother again.

SEVENTEEN

A few days after the funeral Grandma decided we all needed to get away for awhile, so she planned a day trip to the mountains, to the little town of Idaho City. Idaho City is in the National Register of Historic Places because it was the Queen of Gold Camps. In 1862 gold was discovered in the Boise Basin and men were drawn to Idaho by the lure for instant wealth.

Prospectors poured into the area by the thousands. Almost overnight, Idaho City became the largest town in the Idaho Territory. It is nestled up in the pine trees, about 40 miles out of Boise. In its heyday the city had 250 businesses including an opera and theater house, music stores, tailors, breweries, bowling alleys, barber shops, bakeries, pool halls, drug stores and saloons.

At one time, a glass of whiskey was cheaper than a glass of water. Men were armed at all times and quick to defend themselves. The winners went to the local jail and the losers were buried in the old Pioneer Cemetery up on the hillside on the far end of town.

Idaho City flourished for the first few years. It even surpassed Portland, Oregon, as the most populous in the Northwest. During the Gold Rush more than 250 million dollars worth of gold was taken from the Boise Basin. Within a few years, gold became harder to find and prospectors left by the droves.

In 1865 fires wiped out eighty per cent of all of the buildings in town. Luckily the town was rebuilt. Some of the early brickwork and wooden architecture still exist. Many structures erected in the 1860s remain standing and represent some of Idaho's most important historical buildings. Much of the boomtown flavor still remains.

You can stroll along planked boardwalks that formerly rang beneath the boots of the early miners, or walk by the Merc where it once cost a pinch of gold to by an apple. We peeked through the bars of the old jail, where desperados carved their names in the wooden walls. Then we visited the Idaho World Building, the old schoolhouse, and the Pioneer Cemetery full of ancient headboards and old antique grave markers.

We also, visited the nearby "Ghost Towns" of Placerville, Pioneerville and Centerville. Idaho has a lot of history and our family always enjoyed learning about its early days.

Idaho is known for her crystal clear rivers and streams. On our way home that day we took time to stop at Mores Creek and check out the water as Grandpa talked about fishing for Rainbow and Brook Trout. Sitting on the bank of the stream, and watching the moving water was very peaceful and relaxing. It was a great day of resting and getting away from everything.

Grandma Suzanne was notorious for finding us interesting places to see around Idaho. One weekend we might end up over in Weiser, at the National Old Time Fiddlers Contest. It is a contest where up to 350 National top fiddlers from all over the world come to compete for National titles.

Next, we might head off in the other direction for the Trailing of the Sheep Festival held in Ketchum, Idaho. That event includes the history of sheep ranching in Idaho and the Basque and Scottish heritage of the region. It is a three-day event that concludes with a parade and a chance to trail with local herders and their sheep as they go through town. The Sheep Festival was a recipient of the Idaho Governor's Award for Outstanding Cultural Heritage Tourism.

We might head over to The City of Rocks to watch rock climbing and see the unusual rock formations; or drive up to Yellow Pine for the nationally acclaimed harmonica contest.

Another weekend Grandma Suzanne had us all go to Pocatello for the Idaho International Choral Festival, which is held at the Idaho State University. They had choirs from Algeria, Brazil, China, Kenya, Nigeria, Romania, Spain, the United States and Taiwan as the world came together in song. My grandmother loved singing, so listening to all of the choirs was something she talked about for weeks.

We would attend the Annual Basque Picnic in Gooding and have barbecued lamb chops, Basque rice, beans, salad and breads. Or we might go to the Soul Food Extravaganza at Julia Davis Park. They would have foods like Jambalaya, fried catfish, Collard greens, and sweet potato pie.

Our family never missed Art in the Park, with artists and vendors from all over the Northwest displaying a variety of foods and crafts. The event is an annual event that is held in mid-September. It has gotten bigger and better every single year.

Ever since my brother and I were little our family has enjoyed going to all of the community events. Our grandparents worked hard at carrying on the traditions that our parents had started. They worked endlessly at uniting us as a family, and in making our lives full and interesting again. Because of our grandparents all of the Idaho adventures that began in our childhood continued on throughout our lifetime.

One of my favorite places to visit was Hagerman, Idaho. It is a small town situated in Gooding County. The fossil beds found in Hagerman make the small town significant not only as a National Monument, but also as a heritage of the world.

Fossil excavations began in the 1930's and several important and valuable fossils have been found in Hagerman over the years. The fossil beds were named as a National Monument in 1988. The 'Hagerman Horse' has been named as the state Fossil of Idaho. It was identified as one of the oldest species of horse of the Genus Equis. More than 30 complete horse fossils and parts of 200 separate horses have been found so far. Fossils of another 220 species of plants and animals have been discovered in the Hagerman, Idaho area too. Hagerman is known for its fish hatcheries, its natural hot water, and its alligator farms.

Down the highway from Hagerman and across the bridge is a beautiful area called Thousand Springs, it is a rocky ridge along the river where hot water pours out from inside the rocks and cascades down the face of the ridge and cools when it reaches the river.

For a great evening in town, our family enjoyed going to the Idaho Shakespeare Festival where you sit near the bank of the Boise River and watch the performances in the outdoor amphitheater. Picnicking on the grassy hillside around the theater is incredible and you are thoroughly entertained by professional theater performances.

In addition to the Shakespeare Theater, we liked to drive up to Garden Valley, and sit out under the stars and see the live musical productions at the Starlight Theater.

Idaho has a lot to offer in the wintertime too. Many people move to Idaho because of its four definite seasons. Winter brings deep snow in the nearby mountains and sometimes a few inches will accumulate down in the valley, but usually within a 24-hour period the roadways are clear and dry and the Boise Valley is rarely snowed in.

You can go skiing or snowboarding up at Bogus Basin Ski Resort, only 20 miles out of town, and people ride snowmobiles, or go cross-country skiing, or snow shoe through the deep powder.

At Christmastime the families of Idaho enjoy the Botanical Garden Aglow. It is an event where hundreds of volunteer's work together to hang thousand of sparkling lights throughout the Botanical Gardens, out by the old Penitentiary. As you walk along through the outdoor light displays your eyes are filled with the fascination of a fairytale. You drink hot chocolate and then huddle with friends and family around the warm burning barrels that are located at different intervals.

It is an experience that children never forget as they listen to the singing of Christmas carols and are greeted by Santa and a live Rudolph Reindeer.

Christmas time in Boise is also a time of giving. My grandparents said that Boise is one of the most charitable towns they have ever been in. Between Thanksgiving to Christmas the entire town contributes food, clothing and toys to the numerous families in need. The community gives food to the food bank, coats to the coat drive and toys to Stuff the Bus and Toys for Tots.

Spring in the Boise Valley is a time of riding bikes and having picnics in the park. It is the beginning of sunny days and an occasional sprinkle of light rain and the planting of gardens.

Summertime in Boise is a time for hot weather and the smell of freshly mowed grass; it's a time of floating down the Boise River or spending time with the family in local pools. A time for backyard barbecues and homemade ice cream, and families enjoy a time of camping, hiking and roasting marshmallows over an open campfire.

Fall is the season of playing in the leaves and taking long walks down the greenbelt. It is a time for watching football and cheering on The Boise State Broncos! Oftentimes the perfect fall weather in the Boise Valley will last clear up through Thanksgiving.

Unlike other cities in the United States, Idaho seldom has tornadoes, earth quakes, blizzards, hurricanes or floods. It is rare for the schools to be closed because of too much snow, and the airport is seldom closed because of bad weather. People are drawn to Idaho for its perfect climate and its relaxed atmosphere. People in Idaho take the time to be friendly. I think that is what attracted my mother and father to Idaho, in the first placc.

EIGHTEEN

School was going great, and so was driver's training. I was busy all of the time. Shayla and I were really starting to become good friends. She was such a nice person; she really helped me get back into the group again. When we all got together and everybody kind of matched up in couples, I always sat by Shayla. She was fun and she giggled a lot so that made me laugh.

Driver's training was a blast. I felt like I had been driving all of my life. It was a little different in a real car than it was when Clay and I played in my Mini Cooper when I was fourteen, it was ten times better.

Shortly after I had started back to school, Mr. Ryan called me into his office and said they were going to test me, and see what I needed to bring me up to my grade level. The next day I took several tests and the teachers said they would know the answers in a couple of days.

On Thursday afternoon Mr. Ryan called me into his office again and said he had a tutor lined up to help me on a few of my weak areas. I turned around and there was my tutor looking straight into my eyes. I just about melted right there in front of Mr. Ryan, I should have known.

Mr. Ryan said, "Will you know Hailie, don't you?"

I stupidly shook my head up and down without taking my eyes off of her. Neither one of us was smiling as we stared into each other's face.

"Are you guys all right?" Mr. Ryan innocently asked.

I cleared my throat and said, "Oh sure, Hailie will be great to work with."

Then we both turned and walked silently out of the room together. "How do you want to do this?" I ask her not even looking at her.

"Shall we study at your house like we used to do?" She said again looking directly into my eyes.

"O.K. that would be fine," I said nodding my head clumsily up and down not taking my eyes off of her soft smiling mouth.

"Great, then my mom can drop me off around 7:30 if that's good for you," She said with a slight smile.

"Yeah, I have driver's training till 7:00, so that would work out great for me," I stuttered. "Or my grandpa could come pick you up if that would be better?" I added.

She smiled, "No, I'm sure my mom will bring me over, so I'll see you at 7:30."

When I climbed in the car with Grandma to go home after school, I felt like I could probably fly home. "Hailie was my tutor. Tyson's Hailie was my tutor. Tyson's girlfriend was coming to my house at 7:30. O.K., I can do this," I thought silently to myself.

I rushed home from driver's training that night and quickly jumped in the shower. I had just finished getting dressed when the doorbell rang. I could hear Grandma visiting with Hailie in the front room and of course offering her some warm cookies.

I walked out into the front room and smiled and Hailie smiled back at me. "I can do this," I kept repeating in my brain. "Do you want to go into the family room?" I asked timidly.

"Sure, that would be a good place to study," Hailie answered.

We sprawled her notebooks out across the coffee table, and got down to business. Hailie was always easy to understand so we accomplished a lot within an hour and a half.

When we were done, she smiled at me from across the coffee table and said, "I like your hair long."

"Thanks," I timidly said looking into her eyes, "I like your hair too."

We just sat there staring at each other for several seconds until Clayton hollered that Hailie's mom was there.

"Hey, thanks for helping me," I said lightly touching her hand.

"I'm so glad you're back, Will," Hailie whispered as she quickly turned around and left the room.

"Bye," I muttered as she went out the front door. "Oh, I don't know if I can do this," I thought to myself as I dropped down on the family room couch.

I sat there quietly staring off into space. I didn't even notice that Clayton had walked into the family room and sat across from me. I was struggling to sort things out in my mind, and I jumped when Clay started talking, "Boy, that Hailie has sure gotten to be good-looking while we were gone. She almost looks like some kind of movie star with her gorgeous eyes and her hair cut like that." He kept on talking, "Who would ever believe she could be so smart and still look like that? I'd go after her myself, if I weren't only fourteen," Clay said smiling. "How did you get so lucky to get Hailie as a tutor?" He laughed, "Did I tell you that Mrs. Bentley was going to be my tutor to help me get caught up?"

I looked at him startled only half listening to what he was saying, "She's my Hailie," I unexpectedly thought to myself, as I continued to look at my handsome young brother. Then I realized what he had said. "When did you turn fourteen?" I asked him.

"About a month ago," he said. "When I was filling out papers for school, the secretary in the office reminded me that I just had a birthday." Clay smiled at me and he said, "I hadn't looked at a calendar for a long time, and up on the mountain I just made X's on each day to count the days. I had stopped looking at the month or the date. So when I came home and checked it out, I realized my birthday was a few days before we got back to Eagle." He grinned, "I counted back the days and I figured it must have been my birthday the day we met that Mr. Albertson's under the bridge down by Julia Davis Park."

I felt really sad for Clayton, because it seemed like everyone had forgotten his birthdays for the past few years, and birthdays used to be very important to our family. As I stared at him from across the table, he didn't seem to be upset. He was just his normal, happy self, sitting there smiling at me. "Fourteen," I said, "I can't believe you are fourteen already." I reached across the table and slapped him on his back and said, "Well Happy late Birthday little brother."

Clay said, "Thanks," then he changed the subject back to Mr. Albertson.

"I wonder how that Mr. Albertson is doing since his old friend died."

"I don't know," I said. "I wonder if his daughters are still alive." I continued on, "They have a missing person's connection on the Internet."

"What was his first name, do you remember?" I questioned.

"Raymond," I think. "No, Ronald or Russell," Clay stuttered.

"Russell, that's it we both shouted at the same time. His name was Russell Albertson," I said excitedly.

"Let's go put his name into the computer," Clayton said already halfway down the hall heading to the computer at my desk. He quickly typed in the questions about a missing person's identity connection and got the information he wanted. Together we remembered all that we could about the strange, lost man that had lived under the bridge for twenty years. We estimated his daughters to be in their late twenties or early thirties, from what he had said about them and we knew he was from somewhere in Oregon. We entered all of the information about Mr. Albertson that we could think of into the website, and decided to wait and see what happens.

Hailie and I studied together at least three times each week. She was a good teacher and I was slowly catching up on every one of my neglected classes. I was content just to be close to her again. We never talked about Tyson or the way things used to be with us. We studied, smiled at each other a lot and occasionally laughed about something stupid I had interpreted wrong that she had taught me.

One night while we were busy studying in the family room, Clay came running in from my bedroom all excited about an e-mail he had just received. It was from a lady who thought she knew a man named Russell Albertson that disappeared from Oregon over twenty years ago.

We went to the computer and Hailie and I watched as Clay wrote back to the lady that had just contacted him. The lady said that she was Carla Haney, and her maiden name was Carla Albertson. She said that her aunt had raised her and her sister after her mother was killed and her father disappeared. Mrs. Haney told us that together with her sister Kathleen they had been looking for their father ever since he disappeared over twenty years ago. Carla Haney wrote that her father had a breakdown when her mother was killed in a car accident coming home from the store when Carla was ten. She said that her mother had swerved to avoid hitting a dog running in the street and she hit head-on with an oncoming pickup. Carla Haney said that her father couldn't cope with the death of her mother because her mother was eight months pregnant with her twin brothers. They had removed the twin boys after the mother was already dead, but Mr. Albertson was so distraught by everything, that he never even went to the hospital to see the twins. She said that her dad had left her and her sister at their aunt's house two days after the funeral, and they never saw him again. She said her father knew they would be safe there because their aunt loved her father, and he was her only sibling. The aunt never blamed him for abandoning them. She raised all four children knowing that one-day he would come back for them. Carla wrote, my sister and my two brothers and I have never stopped praying that we would one day see our father again. So, as I sit here writing to you a complete stranger, my hopes are high, that the Mr. Russell Albertson that you have described is the same Russell Albertson that we have been searching for all of these years. Could we possibly come to Boise to meet you and Mr. Albertson in person?

Clayton looked at me, "What should we do Will?"

"Of course they can come," I shouted. "Clay, I think we found that poor man's family. I'm just sure of it, and he doesn't just have two daughters he's blessed with two sons too!" I grabbed Hailie and hugged her and jumped up and down, I was so excited.

Hailie was startled by my instant show of affection, so she cautiously said as she breathed into my collarbone, "Will, who is Mr. Albertson? And why are you trying to find his family?"

"Oh he's a guy that lives under the bridge down by Julia Davis Park, and he is all alone because his friend Hank died and they took him away in a white van, and nobody cared about Hank but Mr. Albertson," I rambled. "And he left his girls twenty years ago and he never saw them again," I continued jabbering.

"Wouldn't it be great if they could all find each other after all of these years?" Clay added.

As I gently released my grip on Hailie, she looked at us like we had both totally lost our minds.

Then Clay and I burst out laughing, "All of this does sound kind of bizarre," I said as I tapped the tip of Hailie's nose and smiled down at her. "I guess you had to be there," I said with a huge grin on my face.

"Hailie your mother is here," Grandma Suzanne shouted from the other room.

Hailie just shook her head as she slowly walked away, "I'll see you tomorrow," she said walking out the front door.

NINETEEN

We made arrangements to meet with the four children of Russell Albertson on Saturday morning at our house in Eagle. They traveled in four separate cars full of people. Each of his children had brought their spouses, and all of their children. They also brought their father's sister and her husband, the aunt and uncle that had raised them.

Seeing all of these people drive up our lane that morning was a little staggering to us. We had no idea how Mr. Albertson would respond. He was used to being all alone. We explained to the family that he had been homeless and living under the bridge for almost twenty years, so we weren't sure what they should expect. They questioned how two wealthy young teenage boys like us, had ever come to meet a vagrant living under the bridge in the first place.

So, I briefly explained to the family our situation, and I rapidly told them how we had lost both of our parents, and we had been trapped at our family's isolated private cabin for almost two years. Then I told them how we were rescued by a helicopter during a forest fire and we had finally gotten back into Boise on a fire crew truck, but we looked dirty and neglected so no one would even talk to us. I tried to explain how we were making our way back home to Eagle, by walking on the green belt, so the police couldn't see us, when we met Russell Albertson living under the bridge.

The entire room was completely silent. They all just stared at me in disbelief as I talked; I guess what I was saying was pretty astonishing for them to understand. Our grandparents also, stood beside us looking like they were in shock as they listened to me trying to explain how we had made our way back home to Eagle. They too were listening to the events that had taken place several weeks earlier. So much of what had happened to us, we never disclosed to anyone. It was behind us, we needed to move forward. I was talking fast trying to act as if none of the things that happened to my brother and I were of any importance to anyone any longer.

But as I looked over at the aunt that had raised this man's family, I saw tears streaming down her face, "You boys know personally how it feels to be all alone in the world," she whispered softly. "That is why you would go to so much trouble to help a poor underprivileged man that had spent a good portion of his life concealed under a bridge." She wiped her nose and dried her tears then she took several pictures out from her purse for Clayton and I to examine. They were pictures that were taken of a young handsome father over twenty years ago. She asked us if they looked at all like the man that we had met a few weeks earlier. Altogether there were at least twelve pictures, all smiling pictures, pictures from a happier time.

I had to be honest with her; the man that we had met was filthy, unkempt and very sad. It was hard for me to say if this could be the same man or not. The man in the pictures had straight white teeth and thick blonde hair. The Mr. Albertson that we met had neglected teeth and he wore an old dirty hat and an old shabby gray coat.

"We know what it is like to lose your parents," I said as I looked over at Clay as he shrugged his shoulders up and down, "But Clay and I can not be sure if this is the same person or not." I went on, "All we can do is take you down to the river where we last saw Mr. Albertson, and you can decide for yourself."

Carla Haney then asked, "Would it be all right if we all prayed together before we left for downtown Boise?" She said, "My husband is a Baptist minister, and he could lead us in prayer before we go to meet the Mr. Albertson that you have described." All nineteen of us stood together in a large circle in the front room of my family's home and prayed for an indigent old man that lived under the bridge near Julia Davis Park. Clayton, Grandpa Bill, Grandma Suzanne and I and this new family that had just entered into our lives, all prayed as one for a man that Clay and I had briefly met on our journey down from the mountain.

I was only sixteen years old, and standing together reverently praying with a group of strangers for a man I really didn't even know, put a whole new perspective on unconditional love. This family had not seen their father for over twenty years and yet they still loved him and prayed for his safe return. Also, knowing that if the man we had described to them were their father, he would be filthy, unkempt and may not even recognize any of them.

I stood in awe as I watched the sincere hope in the faces of each person standing in my front room. I suddenly shuddered as I thought how I too would give anything to see my parents alive, just one more time. So, I guess I could understand why this family had never stopped looking for their loved one.

I understand because if I hadn't known where my parents were buried, I would have never stopped looking for them either. What an overwhelming blessing it would be for Clayton and I to be a small part in reuniting this wonderful family back together. In our struggle to get back home, maybe we could somehow help Mr. Albertson to find his way home too.

We finished praying and we then all loaded into several vehicles and somberly headed down to the river. We reached Julia Davis Park at about 11:15. Clayton and I climbed down under the bridge where we had slept the first night we were back in Boise. After weeks of sleeping in my comfortable home again, it was hard for me to realize that I had been forced to hide away in that dirty old cold bridge structure, but I knew that I had.

I shouted for Mr. Albertson, but there was no reply. So, I shouted again. Clayton climbed down to where we had last seen Russell Albertson, but there was no one there. All that he found was an old hat and a worn out pair of gloves, but there was no one around.

We instantly saw the disappointment in the faces of the Albertson family as we climbed out from under the bridge. "I'm sorry, he's not there," I sadly told them as I stood up and dusted off my Levi's.

As we turned around to get back into the vehicles the old man that lived under the bridge, crept out from behind the bushes where he had been hiding and studying us. He had been watching us crawling around in his living quarters and he became agitated and began to holler at us to leave.

Suddenly, his whole demeanor changed, and he started creeping over towards one of the cars. Apparently, he recognized the older women standing near the white van. "Rebecca, Rebecca" he shouted in a revered whispered voice! "Is that you?" He scrambled over to where the aunt was standing and he fell on his hands and knees wailing and clutching his filthy gray coat. He started moaning as he rocked back and forth on the ground, "Oh Rebecca, I'm so sorry, I'm so sorry, can you ever forgive me?" He pleaded as he focused on his sister. She was the only person he recognized after twenty years. He never even noticed the rest of the family standing around him, because they were all small children the last time he saw any of them. They were now adults, so no one else looked the same, but she did. I could tell by his actions that he didn't know that all of these people were even together, because he was only paying attention to his sister.

I watched in amazement as the Aunt, who had raised this man's children for him, fell down on her knees beside him and hugged him tightly. She held this filthy, unkempt homeless person in her arms and whispered with tears streaming down her face, "I already have forgiven you." She gently rocked the old man back and forth in her arms as they kneeled together on the ground. "Russell, we have come to take you home," she quietly said. "Our prayers have finally been answered." It was then that he looked around and noticed all of the other family members gathering around him, each with tears smearing their faces. He looked frightened as he quickly jumped up ready to run. Luckily, Carla's husband was a big brawny man and he grabbed Mr. Albertson before he could flee.

Poor Mr. Albertson crumbled to the ground in a helpless heap, I'm sure he was embarrassed by the filth and impoverished conditions his family had found him in.

Clayton, my grandparents and I stood back and watched as Mr. Russell Albertson, a penniless vagrant from under the Capitol Blvd. Bridge, was patiently introduced to his wonderful, loving family.

With tears of gratitude and hugs from every one of them, we said goodbye to Mr. Albertson's family and promised to get together again within the next few months.

My family just stood there happily waving goodbye as the Albertson family drove away from the park that day, and headed back to Oregon with their newly-found father.

The four of us stood perfectly still for several minutes, we were stunned, we just watched as our new friends drove completely out of sight. None of us moved. We were overwhelmed by the events of the day. Finally Grandma said, "Who's hungry? I think this calls for a celebration, let's have Grandpa take us out for lunch."

I sat silently in the backseat, all the way to the restaurant, fighting back my emotions and thanking the Lord for the eternal love of a family. "I wonder if in twenty years I will still miss my parents," I thought to myself.

Shortly after we got home that afternoon, we received a call from Mrs. Henning, Dad's old secretary. We had forgotten to go visit her as we had promised we would do, and it had been several days since she had come to the open house and to my parent's funeral. Grandma apologized for our negligence, but she told her how busy we had been, getting things settled since Clay and I had started back to school. We promised to call her in the next week or so and set up a time to drop by her house.

Again we got busy and forgot to ever contact her, and when the weekend came, we headed for the Sawtooth Mountains up near Stanley and none of us ever thought of Mrs. Henning again. We drove up to Redfish Lake and stayed at Redfish Lodge. Idaho has breath-taking mountains. There are 2,939 mountain peaks in Idaho; the highest peak is Mount Borah, over by Mackay, it is 12,510 feet above sea level.

My mother loved the Idaho Mountain ranges. Living in Idaho was completely the opposite of when we lived in Florida. Florida has the ocean with its gorgeous sandy beaches, but Mom loved living so close to the mountains and all of the lakes. We would often go fishing at Deadwood Reservoir, Hayden Lake, CJ Strike Reservoir or Hell's Canyon. Everything was so close. We could get to the mountains and many of the lakes within minutes of leaving our house in Eagle. Idaho truly was an outdoor paradise.

Mr. Albertson's family continued to e-mail us on a regular basis. They could not thank us enough for helping them find their father. They said that Russell Albertson was frail and quiet, but the family was relieved to have him home safely where he belonged. Carla Haney told us that she had moved her father in with her and her husband and their three children. She said that it will take some time, but she feels that they will all learn to be a family again. She told us that Russell Albertson was only

58 years old and when he disappeared, twenty years ago, he was the Principal of the grade school.

"He was the Principal of a school?" Clay commented after reading the e-mail. "No wonder he was so shocked when you called him sir." "Remember he told you that no one had called him sir for a very long time?" Clay reminded me. "I would have never guessed that he was once someone important," Clay continued, sounding very puzzled, as he stared out into space.

TWENTY

We had only been back at school for a couple of weeks, and I got a memo about a field trip that the junior high and high School kids would be taking the following weekend. My friends said the trip had been planned for quite awhile, but Clayton and I were not at school when it was first discussed so we didn't know anything about it. They said that one of the guys from the senior class had lost his grandfather during the summer. His grandfather had been a great supporter of our school and before his death he had arranged a special one-day field trip for all of the older kids in the school.

The grandfather had been raised over near Arco, and he was very proud of the area. He wanted the junior high and high school students to experience the unique types of scenery that Idaho had to offer. He had arranged for us to take buses for a picnic and nature hike to the Crater's of the Moon National Monument, and also to go visit the Shoshone Ice Caves. It was early October, and the weather was getting cooler so the fall colors should be out in full bloom. We were advised to take jackets and pack a lunch and to have some money to buy dinner, because we would be gone the entire day.

We planned to leave the high school at 7:00 a.m. Saturday morning and not return until around 9:00 p.m. that evening. Clayton and I had never been to Crater's of the Moon so we were anxious to go see that area. Mom and Dad had always talked about going there, but we never got any closer than Sun Valley.

The memo said that the grandfather had lived in Idaho all of his life and that he had been raised on a huge cattle ranch out near Craters of the Moon when he was growing up. Six of his grandchildren had attended our school and he wanted to do something special for the teachers and the students, because the school had done so much for his grandchildren. He had written a letter to Mr. Ryan saying that he felt it would be a real learning experience for the students to go see some of the unique lava rock formations and ice caves that Idaho was so famous for.

Bright and early Saturday morning Grandpa drove us to the school to get on the bus. Clayton didn't ride the same bus as I did, but Michael, Shauna, Duke, Juliana, Shayla, Tyson and Hailie did. We had a blast! We laughed, told stories on each other and just acted like sixteen-year-old teenagers. The trip over would have been kind of boring if I hadn't been sitting with all of my friends, because everywhere you looked it was all farmland or desert. We passed through several small towns and then it was back to the desert again. We were having so much fun we never even noticed where we were going. Even Tyson was laughing along with us.

158

He didn't seem to be as threatened by me as he was when I first got back home.

We started talking about when we were all in Junior High and we decided it was time to start up our band again. None of them had played together since I disappeared two years ago, so they would be just as rusty as I was.

We arrived at Crater's of the Moon National Monument and Preserve around noon, so the first thing we did was head for the picnic tables over by the parking lot.

After lunch it was time to go hiking. I was absolutely overwhelmed by everything I saw. The park was phenomenal. It was established in 1924 and it had three major lava fields that covered approximately 400 square miles. All three Lava fields lie along the Great Rift of Idaho with some of the best examples of open rift cracks in the world, including the deepest known on earth at 800 feet. There are excellent examples of basaltic lava as well as tree molds lava tubes (a type of cave) and many other volcanic features.

Of course I appreciated all of the historical facts, and learning the statistics of how things had come into being. The entire park was unbelievable; there were huge black rocks everywhere. It was like walking on the moon. It was one enormous volcano. I had never seen such cool terrain in all of my life. Everywhere you looked everything was black. We walked on cinder trails that went through the rocks and up past giant craters. We climbed through caves and over giant boulders that were larger than a house. I had never seen anything like that before in my life. I gazed out over the black rocks from one of the open viewing areas and thought of all the wonders of nature that Idaho had to offer. For me

Crater's of the Moon had to be one of the most spectacular places of all. The grandfather who sent us on the field trip was right; it was a very educational place to see. I wondered if this would top the Bruneau Sand Dunes for Clayton. That had always been his favorite place to go.

Shayla and I hung out together quite a bit at Crater's of the Moon. Everyone acted like she was my girlfriend, and that was all right. She was nice, pretty, and funny, and she made me feel good about myself. We were together when we walked through the Shoshone Ice Caves too, and we laughed and teased each other, and of course Shayla giggled. I loved her giggle. When she laughed, she made me laugh. She was fun to be around.

The Shoshone Ice Caves were actually closed for the season, they were only open until late September every year, but they had a special tour just for our school. One of the things that they told us, was that it didn't matter how warm or cold it was outside, it could be 100 degrees, but the cave remains 30 degrees Fahrenheit at all times. They had extra coats hanging at the entrance door for people to put on before entering the ice cave.

They said that in the early 1940's the entire cave melted because the natural opening was modified. In 1950 a family named the Robinsons acquired the cave and they studied the cavern, charted the airflow through the passage, and restored it to its icy state in 1962. As you walk along through the ice caves, you follow several hundred yards of wooden walkway that is only a few inches above the ice. If you stand on the walkway and remain perfectly still, you realize how quiet, barren and cold it is in the cave. Shayla and I talked quietly as we walked together through the cave; we couldn't believe that there could be a frozen ice cave hidden deep inside the Idaho desert.

Idaho truly was a place of wonder. It had something for everyone. Mom loved the mountains, Dad loved the trees, Clayton loved the Sand Dunes and I was in awe of the giant black rocks of the Craters of the Moon.

I sat with Shayla when we stopped for dinner in Twin Falls, and of course we planned to sit by each other on the bus ride all the way home. We talked and laughed, she was so easy to talk to. I was a sixteen year old teenager, and Hailie was with Tyson; so from that trip on Shayla and I were a couple. It felt comfortable having a girlfriend again. It was nice belonging with someone. Someone I could talk to and that was easy to be around.

After we finished dinner in Twin Falls and got back on the bus and headed towards home I suddenly recognized where we were, and I realized that Clay and I had been in that area before. Several years earlier our parents had taken us to watch an outdoor concert in Jackpot, Nevada, about sixty miles past Twin Falls.

I remember the concert was out in the sun and it was hot, crazy and loud but Clay and I loved it. Later on that night we ate at the Cactus Pete's buffet. Our family had traveled all over the world, and we had eaten in a lot of incredible restaurants, but we all agreed that the Canyon Cove Buffet at Cactus Pete's Casino was the best buffet we had ever eaten. We had giant crab legs, shrimp, prime rib, ham, and all types of fish, clams and fresh oysters. Clay ate at least six desserts from their elegant specialty desserts section. They offered desserts like little cut up cheesecakes with dainty butterflies painted on the top, or cute little cream puff swans and gourmet cakes and pies and crème brûlée. Dad savored the gooey caramel apples and Mom went back twice for the bread pudding with hot caramel sauce. Our whole family raved about the restaurant's extraordinary food. After dinner we left Jackpot and went back to Twin Falls to spend the night, because our family was going to another concert the following day. We often talked about driving back over to Jackpot to have dinner again, but we never did.

The next morning we left Twin Falls to go to the Malad Gorge State Park to see the other concert. As we were leaving Twin Falls we had to cross the Perrine Bridge, it is one of the highest bridges in the world. The Perrine Bridge is a four-lane highway on US 93 that connects Twin Falls to Interstate 84. The bridge is 1,500 feet long and it is 486 feet above the Snake River. In 1927 it was the highest bridge in the world. It is one of the only man-made structures in the United States that allows base-jumping from the bridge all year long.

In 1974 Evel Kneivel attempted to jump a motorcycle across the canyon on the South rim, but he failed.

I remember after we crossed the Perrine Bridge that day we got on the freeway and headed towards the Malad Gorge State Park. The Malad Gorge State Park is a 652-acre state park that was formed by lava flows and melting glacier run-off. The Malad Gorge is about 12 miles long and the footbridge over the gorge from the river is approximately 150-175 feet high, but the canyon deepens to 250 feet near the Snake River Canyon.

The concert that we went to was called, Jazz in the Canyon at the Malad Gorge. It took thousands of years to create a theater worthy of such an event and Jazz in the Canyon is one of Idaho's biggest summer events. Our family enjoyed being a part of all of the wonderful festivities.

I really liked the area around Twin Falls, and I didn't realize our school field trip would end up there. I remember Mom commenting about the Shoshone Ice Caves, whenever we were near Twin Falls, but we never took the time to drive over to see them. So, I was really glad that we finally got to go see the ice caves on that field trip.

Hailie continued to be my tutor even after I started going out with Shayla. We still studied three nights a week and I reminded myself that I was just her student and she was my teacher. I was amazed at how smart Hailie was in every subject that we studied. She was so patient and considerate to help me to catch on. She was so advanced for someone her age, I was lucky to have her there to help me. I knew it wouldn't be long before my test scores would be back up to my age level and I wouldn't need her help anymore.

One night as we were studying, I was suddenly panicked when I glanced over at Hailie's soft, innocent face, and for one quick moment I realized that when I was all caught up with my studies, I would no longer meet with her three times a week. She looked up at me and smiled her sweet gentle smile, as if she were reading my mind. I had to quickly look away for fear she would be able to tell what I was thinking. Although she was Tyson's girlfriend and Shayla was mine, I always looked forward to our time together. It was like it used to be, just the two of us studying, talking and being best friends.

With so many drastic changes that had gone on in my life in the past couple of years, having Hailie by my side, even for a few hours each week made things seem more normal. As I watched her get ready to leave that evening I struggled with a plan to keep her meeting with me, but I wasn't sure what to do. I knew that because of her help, all of my grades were back up to A's again in all of my classes.

The following weekend the girls in my class were having an all night birthday party for Duke's girlfriend, Juliana. Her parents said that absolutely no boys could come by to crash the party. The girl's were going to stay up all night and watch chick flicks and eat pizza and popcorn and do girl stuff, so no boys were allowed.

That worked out for me because on Saturday morning our family took off on one of our all day Idaho culture adventures to see Massacre Rocks State Park. The park had a lot of history; we read that as travelers on the Oregon Trail passed by the Massacre Rocks State Park area they inscribed their names and the date on a rock called Register Rock. The park is around 900 acres and it contains about 300 species of plants and around 200 species of birds.

TWENTY ONE

On Tuesday morning while I was away at school Grandpa's lawyer and accountant from Florida arrived in Boise. They came to settle up all of the debts and expenses that our family had accrued over the past two years. All of the funeral expenses and the cost for the helicopter rescue team were in, and it was time for the men to put everything in order. The money from the insurance company had been settled and my grandfather's two advisors, Mr. Brooks and Mr. Jennings came to take care of all of the debts.

They would start by paying off all of the atrocious expenses from the rescue team for finding and bringing my parents down from the mountain. Next of course they had the funeral expenses to take care of; then they would pay back all of the money taken from my grandparent's savings accounts that had been used to keep our family's affairs in order for the past two years while we were gone. It was decided that they would pay off the house in Eagle so that the property would be debt-free. After all of the checks were written and the debts were all paid in full, the two men gave my grandfather a handsome bill for their hours of service.

Then they set up a college savings account for Clayton and I for the future. The rest of the insurance money was distributed into several large savings plans. They knew that Clayton and I would never need to worry about money again for the rest of our lives.

When we got home from school that day everything was ready for our signatures. Even with Clayton and I being under age my grandfather's two advisors wanted to make sure we read and understood everything that had been discussed.

Grandpa fully trusted Mr. Brooks and Mr. Jennings so that was good enough for me, but I still read through all of the documents extensively like they advised. I knew I would be seeing these two men at least twice a year, because they would still be handling all of our family's affairs.

As I carefully read over all of the information they had handed me, I was shocked when I read how much money was being redistributed back into my grandparent's savings accounts. They had spent thousands and thousands of dollars taking care of everything while our family was away. For as long as I live, I could never thank my grandparents enough for all that they had done for my mom, dad, Clayton and I.

After the two men left I told my grandparents how grateful I was for everything they had sacrificed for my family. I also, added how much I appreciated them for insisting I bring my parents down from the mountain to be buried in a cemetery. I will forever be indebted to my grandparents for their never-ending love and their priceless wisdom.

TWENTY TWO

Shayla and I saw each other at school every day and we talked on the phone every night. One night as we were talking, she started telling me about how upset everyone had been when my family disappeared. That was the first time anyone had told me all of the details about what people had done for us after we were gone.

She said the kids had put up posters all over town, and in every surrounding town within 200 miles. The parents had taken turns driving the groups of kids to all of the surrounding areas. They set up a hotline and posted pictures on the Internet asking if anyone had seen our family. She told me that Michael, Duke and Hailie talked to my grandparents every day, sometimes five or six times a day just sharing ideas and trying to figure out what to do next.

Shayla told me about the private investigators that my grandparents had hired and she said they had come to the school and Mr. Ryan had let them talk to every student. She said there had been hundreds of volunteers that had searched for us for several weeks after we first disappeared.

Shayla started to cry when she told me that our ninth grade class along with several of the teachers and some of the parents had held special prayer meetings at 6:30 a.m. every morning for over three months, praying for my family to be found.

She went on, "Will, we were desperate and we didn't know what to do." She said, "We couldn't believe that no one saw you guys leave town." She was crying so hard that I could barely understand what she was saying, "We felt so sorry for your grandparents, they had put up rewards for anyone who knew anything about your family's whereabouts." Shayla said, "But no one saw anything, and as far as I knew they never got any leads from anywhere."

Shayla was really honest and she felt she needed to tell me about Hailie. She said, "Hailie was so upset when no one could find your family that she finally had to go for counseling. She cried all of the time and she stopped doing her school work. The teachers didn't know what to do with her, because school had always been so easy for her and it had been the most important thing in her life."

Shayla got real quiet for a minute, then she said, "Will, I was really worried about her and so were her parents." She said, "Hailie met with the church counselor five afternoons a week. They prayed together and he listened to her talk about your family." Shayla went on, "Because I was Hailie's best friend she would sometimes tell me things that they had talked about. Hailie is so smart and I think it's because she is so intelligent and she is such a deep thinker that she couldn't handle your family being gone. It was completely out of her control, and she couldn't understand how you could just vanish and she couldn't figure out a way to solve your disappearance."

Shayla got really quiet again, "She prayed and prayed but you never came home." Then Shayla told me something I couldn't believe, "Her family finally took her away for several weeks to the Oregon Coast to try to get her to refocus. It was so weird Will, you guys were only fourteen, but she acted like you were twenty."

I was stunned by what Shayla was telling me. I didn't know what to say or how to even respond to what she was saying, because I knew in my heart my fourteen-year-old Hailie Loo was all that kept me going when I was trapped up on Moon Mountain.

The words that Shayla told me haunted me for several days, and I couldn't even look at Hailie in the face. I was so sorry that my disappearance had caused her so much grief. Apparently, she had lost the same two years out of her life, as I did out of mine.

TWENTY THREE

I finally, got my driver's permit and I could drive as long as I drove with an adult in the car. It was so great. It wouldn't be long until I could drive on my own, but for several nights I woke up horrified about my reoccurring nightmares of my dad riding in my car with me. The loss of my parents continually haunted me.

My life was full and happy, my grandparents were great, but I constantly missed my parents. The day I finished driver's training I wanted to rush home and tell my mom, but I had to catch myself and remember she wouldn't be there when I got home.

We started practicing our band again and it was really coming together. The guys had football practice every night except Wednesday, so we tried to practice then. I was anxious to be on the football team again, but with tutoring and driver's training, I didn't have the time, so I decided to put it off until the next year.

Our family still loved football, so Clayton and I and my grandparents went to every school game and most of the Boise State games that we could get a ticket for. My grandparents did everything to make our world as ordinary as possible.

One Friday night there were no games, so all of the guys were coming over so that we could practice our band. Hailie rode home from school with me so she could help me finish up the last of my tutoring before band practice. I dreaded coming to the end of our study time together, because I knew it also meant we would no longer see each other all of the time. I owed her so much, but I always guarded what I said to her. I knew that she was Tyson's girlfriend and I honored that, and of course I was with Shayla.

Our friends started to arrive shortly after Hailie and I had finished studying. Grandma Suzanne had fixed homemade pizza and salad for everyone. It was going to be a time to celebrate: I got my driver's license, I finished my tutoring classes and our band was back together again. Shayla, Shauna and Juliana came over too, so it was going to be quite a party.

When everyone had finished eating we all got up and headed towards the family room to go start practicing. Before we could get started my grandpa walked in from the pasture and asked us if we would help him for a few minutes with the plywood on the barn. The guys all said they would be glad to help, and we followed him out to the outbuilding. No one had been in the barn since we moved back home. In fact the plywood was still up on the doors and windows from over two years ago when the contractors had sealed everything up. We had never bothered to take any of it down when we removed the rest of the plywood from the house and other buildings.

We didn't need the barn, so we had just left it all boarded up. I knew it would only take a few minutes with all of us helping him, and then we could get back to our band practice.

Michael, Shauna, Duke, Juliana, Tyson, Clayton, Devon, Shayla, Hailie and I all followed Grandpa and Grandma out to the barn. One by one we unscrewed each screw and started removing the plywood. The more I thought about it the more it puzzled me why my grandpa was removing it at that time, but I guess he was just taking advantage of having so many guys there to help him. Within a few minutes the plywood was down, and we quickly turned around to head back to the house to start practicing.

As we were leaving the barn, Grandpa asked me if I would go in and turn on the barn lights for him to see if they worked. I was starting to get irritated, but I quickly did as he asked, and I opened the door and flipped on the switch. The lights worked fine, so I hurriedly turned around and started to head for the house, when something caught my eye over in the far corner of the barn. I couldn't tell what it was, because it was covered up. I was surprised, because I thought the barn was empty, so without hesitating I walked over and slid the cover off of the object on the other side of the barn. My heart stopped beating. I couldn't believe my eyes. I rapidly turned to my grandparents who were standing in the doorway with all of my friends, and I questioned, "But how?" I stammered.

"The man from the tow truck brought your license plates back to the house three days after you disappeared, and so I bought your car back from him," my grandpa said with a cracking voice and huge tears running down his face.

"I know how much that old T-Bucket meant to your dad and I when we built it together." Grandpa stuttered, "There is nothing like the bond between a Dad and son and his first car." Grandpa went on fighting continual tears running down his face, "Will, it's not that the car was so valuable, but it's because your dad had picked it out just for you, so I couldn't let it be repossessed. I knew how much that little Mini Cooper meant to you and your dad. Your dad had those flames professionally painted on the front fenders and he was so excited he could hardly wait for you to see them.

Your dad had called me in Florida twelve times in three days telling me about how excited he was about that little Mini Cooper. He told me about the special chrome rims and wheels he had purchased for it. He had a car painter airbrush the blue and orange translucent Boise State flames that burst out from around the headlights and the front tires. Your grandma and I couldn't help but get caught up in all of the excitement. Surprising you with that little yellow car was all your dad could think about for the several weeks before your birthday." Grandpa looked over at Grandma Suzanne, "That's why we got you those personalized license plates. Your parents were so excited about your birthday, and we wanted to be part of the surprise too."

Grandpa sighed and looked down at the barn floor, "If the tow truck driver hadn't brought your personalized plates back to the house, at the exact time that we were here, we would have never even known your car had been repossessed."

I then looked over at my grandma Suzanne who was sobbing and covering her face.

"The car has been safely waiting here in the barn for you since three days after you left home," my grandpa said sadly as he tried to smile.

I was in shock as I turned around to look at my friends. They looked as shocked as I felt, but my eyes focused only on Hailie as she came running across the barn and leaped into my arms crying into my collarbone. "My car, it's my car Hailie," I said quietly into her hair, "My Grandpa bought my car back, I can't believe it. It's the car my parents picked out for me." I fought back my agonizing emotions because I didn't want my friends to think I was a big baby, but I lost it when I looked over at Michael and Shauna and saw them smiling with huge alligator tears running down their faces.

"It's my birthday present, Hailie," I said softly stroking her hair. "I loved my car so much because my parents bought it for me."

"I know," she whispered, sobbing and shaking her head up and down, "Will, after all that you have been through, you deserve to get your little Mini Cooper back."

I then looked up and glanced over at Tyson, he didn't look very happy with me. But Shayla, sweet, sweet Shayla then walked over and hugged me, just like Hailie did, and Tyson seemed to calm down. Shayla always seemed to know exactly the right thing to do, at the right time. She was such a wonderful friend to me. She always had been since we were in grade school.

I stood there for several seconds staring at my awesome little Mini Cooper. Then I slowly walked over and gently ran my hand across the hood of the car. I knelt down on my hands and knees next to the orange and blue flamed fenders; it really was my car. I couldn't believe my car had been parked in the barn all of that time.

I slowly stood up and carefully covered the little mini back up with the car cover. I got my composure and I turned around and smiled at my friends and said, "Hey, let's go play some music." They headed for the door and I slowly turned off the barn lights while still staring at my little car. Then I happily followed my friends into the family room to start practicing.

"So, that's why Grandpa asked us to work on the barn at that time," I thought to myself. "My friends were all there when I was fourteen and I first got my little car and he wanted them all to be there when I got my car back!"

That night I couldn't sleep, so I got out of bed around 3:30 a.m. and went out to the barn. I turned on the barn lights and carefully uncovered my car. Then I slid in behind the wheel of my cherished little yellow Mini Cooper with the bright orange and blue flames dashing out from the front wheels and fenders. As I sat there reminiscing of that special fourteenth birthday, I also thought back to the day when they came to take that little car away from my family. That day was the final breaking point for my father. When the bank came to repossess my birthday present, my poor distraught father just couldn't take anymore. He was so despondent and embarrassed. He just gave up. He irrationally drove us up to Moon Mountain and just left us there. I knew in my heart that the tormented father that died on the mountain that day was not the same dignified father, who had given me my Mini Cooper a few months earlier. I put my head in my hands and sobbed out loud, "Oh I miss my real Dad so much." I leaned my head back on the headrest for several more minutes, and then I bowed my head and silently thanked the Lord for giving me back the extraordinary gift that my parents had chosen just for me, on that magical fourteenth birthday a happier lifetime ago.

The next morning Grandpa had a mechanic over to the house to check out everything on my little car. The mechanic changed the oil and charged up the battery. Although, there were very few miles on my little mini it had been sitting patiently for over two years and it needed to be checked over.

When the mechanic was done, Grandpa, Clayton and I took my little car out for a spin for the very first time. It was fantastic! Driving my own car was even better than I had ever imagined it would be. But I got cold chills up and down my spine as we were traveling down Eagle Road. Grandpa said, "This engine is sure quiet, it just purrs and you are a great driver, Will." I was stunned by what Grandpa had said to me, my mouth flew open and I quickly looked over at him, but he was just smiling and looking straight ahead. I couldn't believe he had said just what my dad had always said in my nightmares, because nobody knew about my dreams, I hadn't ever told anyone.

The three of us drove all over that day. I took them up to Diversion Dam and then on up to Lucky Peak. The highway took us to the top of the hill, and then we stopped for lunch at The Hilltop Café before heading on up towards Idaho City. The road was really exhilarating as we swooped in and out on every curve. It was a beautiful drive and my little

Marilynn J. Harris

car handled like a gem. It was just us; the three Richardson guys enjoying a day of cruising and a special time of male bonding.

TWENTY FOUR

Later that night as Shayla and I were talking on the phone she started telling me about the night of Juliana's birthday party. She said, "The girls had stayed up all night talking and watching movies and the more tired they got, the more they would talk. By about 4:00 in the morning, they all started to talk about you, Will. The girls all voted and they decided that you were the most perfect guy that they know." She kept talking, "You are tall, muscular, and handsome and we all just love your hair. We were talking about how courteous you are and we had to agree that you are different than most of the other guys at our school."

I was starting to feel very uncomfortable. I knew Shayla was trying to be complimentary, but I don't think she realized how much I struggled with trying to fit in and be just like all of the other guys. My life had not been normal. I had been forced to watch both of my parents die and my little brother and I had spent two years trying to stay alive, and the last thing that I wanted to be was different than everybody else.

She went on, "We decided that while you were up on the mountain you really changed. It's a good kind of change, but you're different than you were when you were younger." Shayla kept on talking even when I didn't reply, "We have all known each other all of our lives and we agreed that you are probably the nicest guy we have ever met."

I was hesitant to even respond, but I finally said, "What do you mean, I've changed?"

"You are so gentle and kind to everyone," she answered. "I can't quite explain it, but you seem so much older than the rest of the guys in our class."

Shayla went on, "You were always a nice guy, but it's different now, you aren't moody or rude like some of the guys in the high school are. You are quiet, thoughtful and reserved." Shayla was so honest and she said, "I think every single one of the girls likes you, and would like to be your girlfriend."

"Was Hailie there?" I timidly asked.

Shayla hesitated, and then she quietly said, "Yes, Hailie was there, but she didn't comment when everyone else was talking. In fact she got up and went in the other room when we started talking about you. I think she might have been crying and she didn't want any of us to see her."

I refused to talk about that party anymore, so I changed the subject and started telling her about our drive up to Idaho City. Shayla and I talked for a few more minutes then we got off the phone because she needed to finish her homework, and we never mentioned Juliana's party again.

After we hung up I sat there in my room, thinking about what she had said. I thought about Hailie, and I wondered why she would have cried when they were all talking about me. Then I thought to myself, "I wish I could just be a normal teenager, but maybe it's too late for that."

Marilynn J. Harris

TWENTY FIVE

We had been in school for several months and during the holidays at a Christmas party at Kennedy's house, Clay decided he liked Kennedy's daughter, Ashlynn. I stood firm on my parent's rules though, and told Clayton he was only fourteen and he was too young to date, but he could call Ashlynn his girlfriend. Ashlynn was cute, and nice and besides he had known her most of his life. I knew my mom would approve because she had always loved Kennedy's twin girls. They were Mom's shopping girlfriends.

A lot had happened since we got back home and I was finally able to drive without having an adult in the car with me, and there was something I had wanted to do ever since I got down from the mountain. Something I needed to do all by myself. I took off all alone one Friday afternoon to go out and revisit the company that my dad had worked for.

It was a long ways from our house, but I knew how to get out there, because I had gone there with my parents many, many times before. It was uncanny driving up to the abandoned building and grounds where I had visited so many times as a child. That building like Moon Mountain had lost its enchantment and grandeur. The security entry gates that had always protected the property from intruders were broken and hanging open and ripped off of their hinges.

The tall chain link fences were cut and they had been rammed and driven through. Most of the fencing was sagging or gone. There was graffiti sprayed on the outside walls and all of the signs were destroyed or painted over. It appeared that every single window in the massive complex had been broken or shot out. There were holes shot into the brick and mortar and large sections of the walls were shattered and crumbling. The once beautiful distinguished building was now a disgrace. The manicured grounds were replaced with acres and acres of weeds, dirt and tumbleweeds. The poor discarded building was no longer kept up or even remembered. My father's once cherished building looked like a war zone.

Because of the total neglect of the property, I was able to drive in through the open gates and park my car right up by the front door area of the once stately building. The huge front doors were not locked or even completely closed, so I could enter the building without any effort at all. The magnificent marble floors that I had sincerely missed and dreamed of walking down again, were now dark, dirty and surreal and smelled of urine.

I made my way through trash and garbage that had been dumped up and down every hallway. There were no friendly faces shouting hello from the surrounding office space, like I remembered as a young child. Instead many of the doors were closed and locked tight and they had been spray-painted with impressive gang signs and graffiti logos.

I felt I had entered into a grotesque movie set with cobwebs, broken glass, and no electricity. The massive halls were pitch-black and frightening as I made my way down the hall to the deserted stairway that led up to my father's private office. For over two years I had dreamed of visiting my father's office again, but never in my wildest thoughts could I have prepared myself for what I had encountered.

With all of the trash and garbage up and down the hallways, I knew my father's extraordinary office would no longer be at all as I remembered it, but I knew in my heart I needed to see it for myself just one more time.

I cautiously made my way up the deserted, dark stairway by grasping onto the handrail and taking one small step at a time. I was climbing in total darkness and I had to hug the wall and slowly be guided up by the grimy handrail to find my way up the stairs. This was the first time in my life that I had even been inside the dingy stairway that led to my dad's office. Before, I had always ridden up in his private elevator. The stairway was spooky and unreal.

I finally reached the top of the stairway and discreetly pushed the door open at the top of the stairs. The outer office looked like it had been ransacked and looted just like the rest of the building. There was trash scattered everywhere like someone had gone through Mrs. Henning's office looking for something important.

The giant doors that led to my dad's private office where left wide open, and I could see inside his once impressive office space. The desk and tables were gone and there was trash strewn everywhere just like in all of the other parts of the building. It was like some moving company had taken the furniture and just thrown all of the important papers and files out onto to the floor and then someone had gone through and destroyed everything in their path. It greatly saddened me to see my father's once magnificent office in such a desperate condition. The safe was left open and everything was gone. The beautiful furniture and the pictures, including my mother's prized giant family portrait were all gone too. Only trash and papers lay scattered everywhere. The walls were cracked and spray painted with graffiti and the room smelled like an old water-damaged hotel.

My mother had told me how two guards had walked my father out to his car one day and told him to leave the premises and never come back. It was appalling to see so much unnecessary destruction done to such a beautiful building.

"Who did all of this damage?" I wondered, as I sadly walked over to the huge broken picture window that at one time, stood opulent behind my dad's exquisite dark-oak desk. As I glanced out the shattered picture window I couldn't help but smile as I recalled how my dad would always tease us, that he could see Moon Mountain from his desk. Clay and I would pretend we could see it too, just to humor my dad. As I stood there reminiscing and staring out of the shattered dirty window, I suddenly coughed from all of the dust and dirt that hung around the room.

It was hard to breathe because everything was so dusty. My thoughts of the past were still scrambling around in my head, and I decided it was time for me to leave when I suddenly noticed movement out near the back of the building. There were teenagers lounging around on piles of trash and old stacked up boxes. They had spiked hair and hanging chains and tattoos. They looked dirty, unkempt and mean.

The hair on the back of my neck stood straight up and I realized I had to get out of there before they noticed me; but it was too late. One of the guys with spiked blonde hair saw me standing by the broken window, he must have heard me cough and he started pointing up my way. Fear crept all through my body, and I suddenly felt trapped. The only way to get out of my dad's office was down the dark, deserted stairway that I had come up on. If this gang of kids knew the building at all, which I was sure that they did, they would know I could not escape without running right into them. I was so scared I couldn't decide what to do, but I knew I had to do something, because I could tell the rest of the group had discovered me standing there.

Most of the window was gone so I could clearly hear them laughing and cussing and shouting horrible words at me. I had never in my life been a fighter, but even if I was to fight them, I was completely out-numbered. As I watched them, I stood at the side of the window so that they could no longer see me, but I could tell they were getting crazier and crazier. I don't know who they thought I could be, and I'm not sure they even cared who I was. They just didn't want me watching them, it made them insanely upset. Then suddenly their hollering got louder and they were shouting and screaming irrationally. Instantly they headed for the door that led to the stairway. I had no idea how many of them there were, but I knew that they were coming for me and there was no where to hide and no way to escape.

I quickly ran over to the giant solid oak doors that once guarded my father's private office, and I slammed the doors securely shut. I barricaded myself inside my dad's old office and quickly prayed, and then I dialed 911. When the dispatch officer answered I explained my situation and I gave her the business address that I had known most of my life. Then I told her that I was trapped inside my father's old office area, on the top floor in building number 8. I had barely finished telling her my name, when I heard the clomping of footsteps running up the stairway on the other side of the locked office doors.

The dispatcher remained on the line and listened along with me, as the furious voices kept shouting and screaming terrible words at me, while they tried to break through the solid office doors. I didn't know who the gang members were or where they had come from, but I could tell whoever they were they were violent and angry and I knew if they got through the solid doors I would be in big trouble.

Within seconds of my call, I could hear sirens coming from every direction. Instantly, the banging stopped and my attackers retreated back down the stairway. I stood to the side of the window again and watched as the wild-looking teenagers fled in every direction. Some of them drove away in old cars, some on motorcycles and many of them took off running through the dessert on foot. They looked like ants scrambling around on a giant anthill.

The dispatcher was still on the line with me, as I inhaled and let out a huge sigh of relief and then I told her, "Thank you, the officers have arrived." I hung up my phone and leaned up against the wall on the far side of the office. I was trying desperately to catch my breath, I was scared to leave, but I was also scared to stay. I didn't know what to do.

Suddenly, I heard firm footsteps coming up the stairs and soon two police officers tapped on the office door and identified themselves. I carefully unlocked the big solid oak doors, planning to be arrested for trespassing.

"What are you doing in this building?" one of the policeman asked me.

"This used to be my father's office and I hadn't been here for over two years and I just wanted to see it again," I said looking shamefully at the floor. "My name is William Richardson and my father was Clinton Richardson, and he was the CEO of this company until it went bankrupt," I continued telling him, still looking at the ground. "I'm sorry sir, I wanted to see my dad's office again," I quietly stated.

"Your name is William Richardson? Is your grandfather Bill Richardson that lives in Eagle?" the officer said.

I quickly looked up and recognized the security policeman that had stayed with Grandma and Clay while Grandpa and I went up to Moon Mountain to find my parent's bodies. "Yes sir," I politely answered. "But Grandpa doesn't know that I'm out here. I came out alone so I could see my dad's old company again," I told him.

I knew that the officer had become good-friends with my grandparents. He had been out to visit them several times since we had gone up to Moon Mountain. He often dropped by for a cup of coffee or to chat with my grandpa. He didn't live very far from our house in Eagle. Grandma said he wasn't married and he didn't have any family in Boise so he would stop by and Grandma Suzanne always gave him warm cookies, a hot slice of bread or a piece of pie with ice cream.

"You know Will, we have had a lot of trouble with gang fighting around this old abandoned building, and several of the kids have almost died," the officer continued. "It's not really safe for a young man like you to be out here alone, I think you better let us walk you back to your car, so we can make sure you can get away all right."

I looked at him and questioned, "You mean you're not going to arrest me?"

The officer replied back to me, "There really isn't a law against a young man visiting his dad's old deserted office."

"Thank you," I said as I glanced back at the big oak doors that led to my dad's private office. There across the left door panel was my dad's nameplate, it had been proudly placed there twelve years earlier. I must have been staring at it, because the policeman noticed what my eyes were focused on and he took some sort of prying device out of his back pocket and gently pried the nameplate off of the door.

The kind officer smiled as he handed me the nameplate and said, "I don't think anyone would mind if you kept this. This poor old building doesn't need it anymore."

I quickly shook my head up and down as he handed me the golden nameplate, then I whispered, "Thank you."

When we got downstairs, we met up with several other police officers. They had scared the gang away for now, but they knew that they would be back. "They must live in my dad's old abandoned building," I thought to myself.

I again said thank you to all of the policemen and climbed into my car to drive away. Before I could leave, the policemen that knew my grandfather shouted to me "Hey, nice car. Great orange and blue flames," the kind policeman stated.

"Thanks," I said rubbing my finger across the letters on the golden nameplate that he had salvaged for me, "My dad bought it for me." Then I headed out to the main road and turned to go out towards Eagle. I had one more stop I wanted to make.

It was already late afternoon when I entered the road to the Cloverdale Cemetery. I slowly drove around until I reached the area where my parents were buried. I got out of my car and walked over to their recently placed headstone. It was a large headstone with my mother's name on one side, and my father's name on the other. I knelt down on my knees and lightly brushed the grass away from the stone where my parents were buried.

"I went out to your office today Dad," I said speaking to the grave marker as if it could hear me. "It doesn't look so good," I went on, "I wanted to go back and just see for myself what things looked like, but it's worse than I thought. Everything is gone."

"You'll be glad to hear, we're all doing fine at home. Grandma and Grandpa do everything they can to make life as normal as possible." I kept on talking, "The house and yard look great, you would be pleased Mom. Clayton and I both got all A's on our report cards, and Dad the Boise State Broncos are doing great again this year." I smiled and said, "Clayton has a girlfriend, it's Kennedy's daughter Ashlynn, but I told him our family's rules were no actual dating yet because he's only fourteen." I added sadly, "Hailie is still going out with Tyson" I stared at my parent's names on the carved stone for a few seconds and then I quietly whispered, "Dad, I really love my little Mini Cooper, thanks." Then I shook my head and went back to my car to head home for dinner.

Grandma had dinner ready when I got home around 5:30. I quickly went to my room to wash up and to hide the golden nameplate that the policeman had given me. I didn't want my grandparents to know that I had been out to my dad's office earlier that day. Visiting my dad's company was a lot more dangerous than I had ever imagined it would be. I know that my grandparents would be horrified if they were to find out the intense situation I had been through earlier in the day. I hid the nameplate so they wouldn't ask me any questions.

I was quite sure the policeman would never disclose the incident to my grandfather. I had not broken any laws, and he seemed like the kind of person that could be trusted.

My grandmother had made a Caesar salad, lasagna, hot French bread and green beans. We had white cake with chocolate frosting for desert. My grandma was such a good cook. I thought to myself, "I could end up 300 pounds by the time I graduate from high school if I don't watch it, but it would be worth it."

Later on that night, Duke, Devon, Clay and I went to the movies then out to the Dairy Queen for milkshakes. When we got to the Dairy queen we saw Hailie there with her family. She came over and sat with us for awhile and we laughed and talked about the crazy movie we had just seen.

As we sat there talking, a brilliant idea popped into my head. I pretended that there were some problems in geometry that I just couldn't figure out. Hailie hadn't been tutoring me for almost two months and I was trying desperately to think of anything that I could to have her help me again. I really wasn't struggling with anything, but I was to the point that I would start flubbing up just to have her around again. She seemed delighted that I needed her help. We planned to get together every Tuesday night around 7:00. I was still going out with Shayla and she was still seeing Tyson, but from that night on we studied every Tuesday evening until we graduated from high school.

TWENTY SIX

WHEN the weather started getting warmer and it was almost springtime, I decided to give Clayton a long awaited Un-birthday present. So many good things had happened to me since we had gotten down from the mountain, and I felt it was time that something good happened to Clayton too. It was time he got his long awaited birthday party. I talked it over with my grandparents and we decided to give him a huge Un-birthday party two weeks from Saturday.

On Tuesday night I asked Hailie to help me plan his big birthday bash. We decided to invite everyone from the junior high and high school classes and Grandpa Bill said we could have the party out in the barn, so there would be room for everyone. Hailie, Shayla, Michael, Duke and I went from person to person, secretly inviting everyone including all of the teachers. We didn't want anyone to be left out. We made sure that everybody knew that it was a surprise party, so that word wouldn't get back to Clayton. My grandparents bought all of the decorations and Grandpa made sure the barn was spotless. Grandma Suzanne and the ladies from her Bible Study, Gertrude, Jeanne, Earlene, Pat, Martha, JoLeene and Margarette made boxes and boxes of cookies and desserts and stored them in the freezer at Gertrude Smith's house. I could not believe that my grandmother's friends were so excited about helping with the food. We were all getting caught up in the magic of Clay's Un-birthday party.

The ladies made plans to get together again the day of the party and prepare the hot food. They planned to make all kinds of little sandwiches, pizza squares, and baby hot dogs. They decided to have giant fruit trays and vegetable trays and several different kinds of chips. The ladies would fix lemonade, fruit punch and coffee. Everyone worked together secretly putting on the finishing touches. It was so exciting, I could hardly wait. We planned to play music on CD's and dance and cram as many people in the barn as we could.

Thursday afternoon, after school, Hailie and I went to Carl's Cycle Sales on State Street to check out all of their motorcycles. I still had the lime-green jacket hidden away in the top of my closet from his twelfth birthday, but I knew it wouldn't fit him anymore.

We went to several motorcycle places to check out what each one of them had available. We looked at motorcycles, helmets, jackets and gloves, but we knew that Grandpa would have to make the final decision, because he wrote the checks.

Clayton had been waiting almost three years for this birthday party and it was going to be the best birthday party anyone could ever have.

Hailie and I had been out shopping for over two hours, so I asked her if she wanted to get a coke or something. We pulled into the Big Bun Drive-in on Overland Road and I handed her my wallet for her to pay, because the window was on her side. As she reached into my old wallet to pull out some money, she also pulled out the picture of her and my mother. At first I was embarrassed, I'd forgotten that the picture was in there, I didn't intend for her to see it. Hailie, always the gracious one just stared at the picture for a minute, then looked at me sadly and gently touched my arm and smiled, then she put the old worn out picture back into my wallet without asking any questions.

That night I again lay awake in my bed holding the worn-out picture of Hailie and my mom in my hand, thinking about the way things could have been. Shayla was my girlfriend, but Hailie and my mom were still my two favorite ladies.

The following Monday, Grandpa and I picked out the coolest CBF 125cc Honda anyone could get, it was loaded. It was a single cylinder, four-stroke engine with a 5-speed transmission, with electric start. It was brand new, just out of the crate and it came in red, black or white, so we chose the cherry red color for Clayton. Grandpa wrote them out a check for everything, and the motorcycle shop planned to deliver it Saturday morning along with the helmet, jacket, gloves and boots. Grandpa and I left that motorcycle store so excited we were floating on air. We could hardly wait for Saturday night.

When we got home Grandma said she would make sure Clay was out shopping with her at the time it was to be delivered. I could barely think of anything else all week long. Grandpa and I kept encouraging each other and giving each other high fives every time Clay would leave the room, I couldn't wait. I reminded myself of my dad. That is what Grandpa had said my dad had said to him, when he bought me my little Mini Cooper.

On Saturday evening about a half an hour before the party was to start, I took Clayton to the store with me to get him out of the house. While we were gone Hailie, Shayla and my grandparents all finished up the arrangements for the party. Everything looked fabulous. They told me later that not ten minutes after we had left the house; the kids started to arrive.

When we returned from the store at 7:15 there were kids everywhere. Clay was shocked and excited beyond belief. It was great! I discovered that night, why my parents always loved giving parties. It was almost as much fun planning someone else's party as it was actually having someone plan a party for you. Clayton absolutely loved his new bike. It was perfect for him. My little brother had waited three long years for his surprise and he deserved it.

It seemed like there were as many chaperones at the party as there were kids. Both of Hailie's parents came, and of course Kennedy and Ron brought Ashlynn and Abby. My grandparent's friends the Smith's and all of the rest of the ladies from her Bible Study came too; and they were having a ball. The Bible study ladies told me that they wouldn't have missed it for the world, and of course I was thankful because they had made all of the food.

Michael and his whole family came, and Mr. and Mrs. Harriss came with Duke and Devon. The principal, Mr. Ryan and his wife and their little girl also came by to celebrate my brother's special party. Several of the teachers came and so did the coaches and their wives, it was fantastic!

I think that every single student from the junior high and high school classes were there, along with several of Ashlynn's friends from her school. Even Mikal, one of Clayton's good friends, came in hobbling along on crutches. He had a broken leg and his mother, Catherine brought him because he wanted to come so bad.

When the music started to play, many of the adults started to dance. It wasn't long before the Un-birthday boy was out there dancing up a storm with his girlfriend, Ashlynn. They were a good-looking couple, and they were both good dancers. It reminded me of when our mother had first taught us how to dance when we were up at the cabin. Our mother was such a great dancer. One by one more couples entered the dance floor.

Michael went up to the front of the room and shouted for everyone to grab a partner and he said, "When the music stops you must change partners and dance with someone new." I started with Shayla then next I danced with Mrs. Ryan, then I whooped it up with Gertrude Smith then next with Andrea, another one of my grandmother's friends and then I changed to a lady named LaDawn, and then Shauna, Michael's girlfriend. We all danced and laughed and danced some more.

I danced with Juliana, Duke's girlfriend, then with a girl named Rosemarie, that went to our school and then on to Hailie. Hailie, Hailie Loo, my Tuesday night study partner and my best friend. Out of all the ladies that I danced with that night, Hailie fit in my arms the very best of all the dancers. We slowly danced in unison as the music played. I could barely keep my eyes from hers as we danced close together with the room then packed with so many people. It was person to person everywhere you looked. Once again the music stopped and she was gone and we each danced with someone new. That night truly was a night to remember for every one of us.

By 11:00 p.m. most of the kids were gone home and Grandpa turned on a floodlight and let Clayton ride his new Honda motorcycle slowly around the field. Clayton had gone riding many times before, out in the desert with Devon's family. The Harriss family had several motorcycles and that's why Clay had wanted one for so long, because his best friend Devon had one.

Grandpa and I could tell that he knew what he was doing the first time he started the bike. He gave it gas just at the right time and he knew when to ease up on the gas, as he went around a corner. We watched in amazement at how well he maneuvered the motorcycle as he gave it more gas on the straight a ways. He also knew how to use the brake, and to keep it balanced, so we knew he'd be o.k. Just watching him that first night he looked like a pro. As much as he hated to put it away that night, by 1:00 in the morning it was late, and it was time for all of us to head for bed.

My little brother went to bed with a huge smile across his face that night, because he finally got his motorcycle. "This was the best day of my life," he shouted as he walked on down the hall to his bedroom.

"I know the feeling," I said to myself as I walked on into my own bedroom.

I took a hot shower and then climbed into bed. I reached over to the nightstand for my wallet and I started to retrieve the old picture of Hailie and my mom, but instead I found a recent class picture of Hailie wedged tightly in front of the old picture of her and my mother. I took it out and saw that she had written on the back of it. It said: To Clinton William

Richardson III. I will love you for infinity. You are best friend, Hailie Loo. I lay on my bed that night impatiently waiting for morning. Because Hailie Loo will love me for infinity! Although, we were not quite seventeen, I knew that I loved her too. Around 4:00 a.m. I finally fell asleep.

Before I was even awake the next morning, I got a call from Mrs. Henning, my dad's old secretary. She said she hadn't been feeling very well and she really wanted to see me. I apologized to her because it had been several months since she last called and none of us went by to see her. I promised I would drop by after church that day and I ask her again the directions to her house.

I got up and got ready for church expecting to see Hailie when I got there, but she wasn't there. Neither was Tyson or his family.

TWENTY SEVEN

After church I took off by myself to go to Mrs. Henning's house. She lived in a nice old house down in the north end of town. I turned off of Harrison Blvd. and drove about three blocks to the address she had given me. Her house looked orderly and neat with a giant front porch and huge pillars across the front. The house was probably built in the early 1900's.

I briskly walked up the front stairs and rang the doorbell. A crippled up old woman hobbled to the door and slowly opened it and let me in. I had to look at her twice to recognize that the thin sickly woman was Mrs. Henning. I had just seen her seven months earlier and she didn't look ill then. "I am so sorry Mrs. Henning," I sincerely said. "Are you all right?"

"No William, I'm not, but let's go in the front room and sit down because I have several things I need to talk to you about. First of all, thank you so much for coming by," she said with a weak smile. "You know I loved your family with all of my heart, your father was one of the kindest people I have ever met in my life, and he was the best boss anyone could ask for." She smiled, "We worked hand in hand together for over ten years and I was one of his greatest admirers." She looked down at her hands folded neatly in her lap and said, "Will, I am dying and it was very important for me to see you before I die." She shook her head lightly as if to clear her thoughts, "I am on a lot of medication and it's sometimes hard for me to think clearly. First of all I want you to know that your family was the most important thing in your father's life." She slowly went on, "Everything he did in his life was ethical and moral, so don't let anyone try to convince you otherwise." She shook her head again, "It was the company that destroyed him." She looked me straight in the eyes, "I would have done anything for him, and when they took him away that day I really thought I would see him within a few days, but I never saw him again."

"Will, I need you to help me with something," she put her hands out for me to help her up from her chair. So, I stood up and reached to steady her. "I need you to help me get downstairs, because I have something hidden for you," she said.

My mind could not figure out what she was talking about. Maybe it was her medicine clouding her thinking, but I gently helped her down the steep old basement stairs and she said she had not been down to the basement for several months.

She slowly guided me over towards the unfinished part of her basement. The area was covered with cobwebs and earth. It had never been completed. Hidden deep inside, between the dirt walls were several blankets covering some strange objects that she wanted me to retrieve. I squeezed through the dirt walls and pulled out the items covered in blankets. When I removed the blankets, I discovered that the objects were also neatly taped in heavy-duty plastic. She instructed me to remove part of the plastic from one of the objects. When I did I discovered one of the expensive, original paintings that had been hanging on the wall in my father's office. Mrs. Henning said, "I retrieved every single one of your father's expensive paintings for you, including your mother's giant portrait of your family."

I slowly turned toward her and questioned, "How did you get these?"

She smiled kind of a sheepish grin and said, "Help me upstairs and then come back and get them and we'll talk." I got her safely settled in her rocking chair, and then I darted back down stairs for the paintings. One by one I brought the expensive paintings up into her living room. I couldn't believe it she had saved every single one of my dad's valuable pictures. Each picture was worth thousands of dollars a piece.

When I sat down in the chair across from her she continued to share with me all of the events of that day when the men had taken my father from his office. "I begged them not to be so cruel to him," she said. "I couldn't believe they were treating your wonderful father like he was a criminal or something." She went on, "They drug him away and paid little attention to me standing there pleading with them and crying, but I heard them say to him that he could never come back in the building again. They told him that everything in his office then belonged to the bank." Mrs. Henning looked at me, "Will, I knew your father was having money problems, he had not been paid for several months, and I knew those paintings were worth a lot of money; and those paintings belonged to him."

She got a strange grin on her face, "I remember when we redecorated his office and he brought in those original paintings, he was so proud of them, because he had bought each one of them as an investment, and the paintings made the office look so polished and professional. He knew they would be safe as long as they were hanging inside of his private office. The grounds were secured with locked gates, and no one could enter without first going through the guarded security gates, and the gates were guarded 24 hours a day."

She continued on, "As soon as they walked your father out of the building that day, I knew he could never come back for anything. So, I quickly removed all of the paintings off of the walls and the pictures off of his desk and rolled them out to my car on the big coffee cart, which he had in his office. I had to really struggle to get the family portrait down because it is so huge, but I was determined and I knew I had to get it down by myself, because there was no one around that could help me."

"I was parked in the back parking lot and once I carefully had all of the pictures secured on the cart, I went down the elevator and out through the back way. No one paid any attention to me. They were all too busy worrying about themselves." I could tell that Mrs. Henning was very pleased with herself as she said, "Actually, I was saving them to give to your father, but I guess now they belong to you boys." Mrs. Henning continued to tell me, "When you work with someone for a long time, they start to become like family. I was so delighted to be able to sneak those paintings out of your father's office for him. It was as if I were taking care of my own flesh and blood."

We sat and visited and reminisced about all of the M&Ms she had given Clay and I when we were little. I told her that I had gone out to see the office building a few weeks earlier. I told her that it was very run down, but I never mentioned that I almost got myself killed by a crazy gang of teenagers living in the building. I visited with Mrs. Henning for several hours that day, and I promised I'd be back to see her in a couple of weeks, but she died three days later, and I never saw her again.

Our whole family went to her funeral, because she had done so much for us, and we knew she was one of my father's closest friends.

We had all of the paintings appraised and then we stored them safely away in a bank vault. They were worth way too much money to have them hanging up anywhere. It was unbelievable that Mrs. Henning had them hidden down in her basement for almost three years. I often wondered what would have happened to the paintings, if I had never gone to see her before she died.

Mrs. Henning helped me so much that day. She helped me by restoring my faith in my father. It was so comforting to hear someone that was so close to the situation, speak so highly of my Dad. I was glad I got to sit down and visit with her for those few precious hours. Although, I always deeply loved and respected my father I still had continual questions as to why all of our lives had been destroyed as a result of his corporation collapsing.

Mrs. Henning knew my father better than almost anyone did, and yet she thought of him as a kind and totally innocent victim. She explained to me how he had tried everything to keep the company from collapsing. As I listened to her talk that day, I realized that he was not only her boss, she also thought of him as a true friend. That says a lot about a person, when the people closest to you stay by your side. I have to remember she also lost her job that day; she could have blamed my father too like so many of the other employees did, but she didn't. My father always said he didn't know how he could ever survive without her, and he was right. She truly was one of God's Treasures.

So much had happened within the few days after Clayton's party that Hailie and I never got the chance to sit down and seriously talk about anything important. I wasn't sure exactly what everything meant, because Hailie continued to go out with Tyson, so I continued to be with Shayla. Hailie still came over on Tuesdays to study, but since we didn't talk about the picture right away, I was too embarrassed to mention it after so much time had passed. So, we never talked about what she had written on the back of the picture. I never figured out how she had gotten her picture in my wallet without me knowing it, but maybe I will ask her someday.

Marilynn J. Harris

TWENTY EIGHT

On one of our sunny Saturday outings we loaded up Clay's motorcycle on a small cycle trailer and headed out towards Murphy. The Harriss family took their truck and motorcycles too, and we planned a fun day of riding and then we thought we could drive up to Silver City just to look around.

The two families traveled over to Murphy and found the designated off-road trail area where we could unload all of the bikes. Then one by one we took turns riding around the desert mountainside. Clay showed me how to ride his motorcycle and I took off kind of slow at first, but after I got the hang of it I think it was probably the most fun experience I had ever had in my life. I loved it! No wonder he wanted a motorcycle for so long.

206

We rode for several hours then we ate a picnic of sandwiches, chips, cookies and lemonade, and it was back to riding again. Duke and I took off and did a little hill climbing on our own. It was so much fun. I don't know when I had ever had such a fun day. I decided I might have to buy me a motorcycle too!

Around 2:00 we packed up all of the bikes and the riding gear so we could head on up to Silver City. It was a dirt road and we knew it might take us awhile to get up there.

Silver City is an old mining town that didn't burn down like many of the other mining towns did, but it still did not become a modern city. The Idaho Hotel in Silver City is well over 100 years old. You can take an historic ride back into history on horseback exploring the Owyhee Mountains, because the little town of Silver City is surrounded by the 8,000-foot high mountain range. The historical town contains about 75 structures that date back to the 1860s. At one time Silver City had a dozen streets, 75 businesses, and about 2500 people and it was the Owyhee County seat from 1866 to 1934.

Silver City had the first telegraph service and the first daily newspaper in the territory in 1874. Telephones were in use by 1880 and the town was electrified in 1890.

There are hundreds of mines that are dug through all of the mountains, and one mine had up to 70 miles of tunnels that were all hand dug. More than 250 mines were in operation between 1863 and 1865. At least 60 million dollars worth of precious metals were taken from the mines. There are no major mines operating in the area today, but Silver City was still a very interesting place for us to visit. Both families enjoyed learning the history of the old town.

After we left Silver City we headed back towards Boise and stopped at Round Table Pizza for pizza and salads. It had been a great day of riding and our grandparents had become good friends with Darren and Sammy Harriss and their two sons.

Another ghost town that Mr. Harriss had told us about was at Rocky Bar in Elmore County. In the nineteenth Century Rocky Bar had over two thousand people living there. Within two years it became the main settlement in the area and it was even considered for the Capital of the Idaho Territory. A fire destroyed the whole town in 1892 and although it was rebuilt it slowly started to decline. It has not had a permanent population since the 1960's. The old town is located about 62 miles northeast of Mountain Home.

Since the death of my parents we have traveled all over Idaho and experienced the unique history and beauty that makes Idaho a charming place to live. I sensed that my grandparents appreciated the peacefulness of living in Idaho more and more each day; because my grandfather once told me that Idaho was a perfect place for people to retire.

TWENTY NINE

The one lesson that I have learned after living through all of the sorrow that the world has given me, is that no matter how fearful or alone you might feel in the depths of your darkness, the Lord will one day provide a rainbow. No life story is perfect, but we must learn to survive the life story that we have been given.

I have oftentimes questioned myself since that horrifying morning that led to the death of my father. That morning was catastrophic. It was the morning when all of the horrendous events of my life started to unravel. I can't help but wonder what if things had gone differently at certain times in my life? What if when I was five years old, I could have convinced my parents never to move to Idaho because it made me too sad? What would I have changed when my family was healthy and carefree and my dad was a big CEO and he was the most important person in the world to me? Would I have lived my life differently if I had known that when I was fourteen my wonderful family would be destroyed? If I had known when our family took that last trip to China that my life, as I had known it, would never be the same again. Would I have begged my family not to go on that fateful trip? Or at fourteen when I could see my parents depressed and struggling should I have held onto them and never let them out of my sight? Could I have change things? What if that night my father drove us up to Moon Mountain, I had refused to go. Could I have changed all of our lives forever? If I had known what my future was going to bring, would I have done things differently? Of course the answer would be yes. If anyone had told me when I was five years old and we left Florida to move to Idaho, that there would be some extremely happy times in my life, but there would also be some unbearable, tragic times too. I don't think I could have stood it. I'm sure if somehow I was told to be prepared for such anguish, I don't think I could have comprehended it, and if I could have comprehended it, it would probably have driven me insane. If I had known then, what I know now, would I have loved my family more? I don't think I could have. My family was the most important thing in the world to me.

I think God's plan for us to live and learn how our life story goes by living it each day; is probably the most sensible plan. We somehow gain the strength to get through our burdens if we take one burden at a time. If any of us knew what tomorrow would bring, I'm not sure if we could cope with the weight of knowing.

As I look back now at the journey I struggled through after losing my parents, I can barely grasp the reality that I actually survived that horrifying time in my life. All I know is that the early years in a child's life, forms them into the person they will one day grow up to be. My godly beliefs and my strong family values were already instilled in me before that momentous day when I was fourteen years old, and my father drove his car over the mountainside. I didn't realize it at the time of his death, but as I look back on my life, I realize it now. That was all of the parenting I would get for my entire lifetime, because within a few months my mother died too, and I was done with my childhood. Everything that I had learned about the unconditional love that unites a family together, I had learned as a child.

THIRTY

Shayla and I went together for over a year and half. She was one of the nicest people I had ever met in my life. We talked, we laughed and we went everywhere together. I loved her family and I became good friends with both of her little brothers. Everything seemed perfect between us. We never argued or got upset with one another. Shayla helped me to survive some the most difficult times of my life after I first came back from Moon Mountain. I would always be grateful to her for that, but no matter how hard I tried, I knew deep in my heart that I would always love Hailie. I loved her when I was fourteen years old and my life was innocent and perfect; and it was Hailie that I thought about when I was all alone on the mountain during my darkest hours. It was Hailie who struggled and missed me the most when I disappeared, and it was Hailie who prayed me back home. It was my beautiful, graceful

Hailie, who was the most excited to see me again when I returned home after two years. It was Hailie who helped me get caught up with my classes so that I could graduate with my friends, and it was Hailie who studied with me every Tuesday night. No matter how hard I had tried, she was the person in my dreams.

Although, I was not quite eighteen, I knew in my heart that I had the same adoration and oneness with Hailie that I saw in the lives of my parents. I can not describe what makes someone love another person. It's just something that is there and you can't run away from it or pretend it isn't real. Even being with someone else does not make it go away. It's a feeling that makes you happy and it fills your thoughts with joy.

She is the first person that you see in a room full people. The way she walks, the way she smiles, and the dimples on her cheek. The way she listens, the way she dances, and the cute freckles on her nose. It doesn't matter if you are thousands of miles away, that special someone is always with you, tucked up neatly in your heart. It's like God has made her perfect and he's made her just for you. Love is something that encompasses your entire being and you can not change it no matter how hard you try.

Tuesday night as usual, Hailie came by to study, but we didn't have a lot of school work to do because it was our senior year, and we usually got our work done during class-time. It was almost the end of the school year and we would soon graduate and be out of school. We finished up the small amount of homework that we had, and I asked Hailie if she would go to Shopko with me and then I would take her home. I needed to pick up a birthday present for my grandpa.

We just walked around the store talking about nothing in particular and laughing as we looked at silly cards in the card section.

I finished purchasing my grandpa's present and we were ready to leave, but as we were leaving the store we passed by one of those quarter bubble gum machines. Hailie begged me to get her some bubble gum, as she wrinkled up her freckled nose and pleaded in her cute little irresistible voice. So, I put in a quarter to get her some bubble gum, but out slipped a small plastic toy container instead. It took us both by surprise, because it was the only toy in the glass bin, the rest of the machine was full of orange, purple or red giant gumballs. The two of us just looked at each other with questioning looks on our faces. Without thinking, I opened the little plastic bubble container and took out a delicate little imitation ruby ring.

I leaned over close to her until we both were face to face and I looked directly into her innocent blue eyes and I whispered with a serious tone in my voice, "You know what this means don't you?"

Hailie slowly shook her head back and forth as she stared directly into my eyes without smiling or moving away.

Then without thinking I got down on one knee and said, "Hailie Loo, I have loved you as my best friend and I will love you for the rest of my life." I confidently blundered on "Will you marry me?" And I slipped the tiny imitation ruby ring on her delicate little finger.

She didn't answer me. She didn't laugh, get mad or make any comment at all. She looked down at the ring and then back at my face, then she turned around and headed out of the store and went out to my car.

Neither one of us said anything all the way to her house. I'm not sure if I even took a breath. We just drove home in silence. When we got to her house she got out and said thanks and quickly ran inside. I sat there for a few minutes thinking; what have I done?

"O.K. genius, she's not even eighteen yet," I thought to myself, "Maybe she wasn't planning on getting engaged tonight." I kept talking to myself "Besides we're not even going out. What was I thinking?" I kept grumbling on and on, "Maybe she doesn't want to marry me. Maybe she just thinks of me as a good friend. We haven't even graduated from high school yet." I kept mumbling to myself as I was driving home. "I didn't mean right now," I tried to convince myself. "I was thinking when we are older. Oh, she must think I'm crazy, she probably won't ever talk to me again," Then it occurred to me, "Maybe it's because I'm still with Shayla." I kept grumbling to myself, "I'll tell her I was just kidding, if she ever talks to me again."

As I pulled into my driveway I feared I might be sick, I was feeling so nauseated about what I had done. "I will never be able to show my face at school again," I agonized. "The worse part about all of this is Hailie will never want to be around me anymore. I know what I'll tell her," I said talking only to myself. "I'll tell her I don't always think right because I was trapped up on the mountain for so long. That's it, that's what I'll say, Hailie will understand, she knows me, she'll probably know that's true." I sat in my car talking to myself trying to decide what all I needed to say to her when my phone jingled, telling me I had a text. It was Hailie. The message read: "Yes, I will marry you, in one year from today. I will finally be Mrs. Clinton William Richardson. I have waited for you to ask me since I was six years old." The text also said, "My mother said you need to talk to my dad."

I read the text over and over again, and then I put my car in reverse and drove off down Eagle Road.

It was almost dark when I reached the lane to the cemetery. I quickly parked my car and flung open the door then I bolted over to my parent's head stone shouting, "Mom, Mom, Hailie said that she would marry me." I kept shouting, I was so excited, "She said that she has waited for me to ask her since she was six years old!" I kept on rapidly talking as if my mom could hear, "Oh Mom she is so perfect." I continued to talk to the headstone, "Thank you for teaching us how to love. That is probably the greatest gift that you and Dad have given to Clayton and I." I sniffed and wiped my eyes, "I know that Hailie and I are young, but because of you and Dad we will never financially want for anything." I continued on as if my mother was sitting beside me, "I promise we will both finish college." I stared at the grave marker, "I promise to make you proud of me." I sat there on my hands and knees for a few more seconds, staring at the names on the cement grave stone, and then I let out a big sigh and silently stood up. Looking down on the graves again I whispered, "Mom and Dad I still love you infinity." Then I turned and walked back to my car and headed on home to Eagle.

Since the day that Clay and I were rescued from Moon Mountain we have traveled to Florida, Israel, Alaska, Maryland, Germany, Oregon, Hawaii, Australia, and we have visited every inch of Idaho. We returned to school to play football, basketball and track. Uniting again with my band will forever be one of the treasures of my lifetime. We have met our cousins in Baltimore and we have visited with our cherished friends in

Oregon, the family of Mr. Russell Albertson. I continue to be one of The Boise State Bronco's greatest supporters; blue and orange blood runs through my veins. I have played golf many times with my dad's best friend, Greyson. I have eaten gooey brownies at Kennedy's house.

I have even met my remarkable friend Mr. Lance Durham, the cook from the fire camp. He was the only person that ever noticed my brother and I when we were first brought down from the mountain. He fed us and paid enough attention to two filthy unkempt indigent boys to track down their family in Florida. Quiet, reserved, Mr. Durham is probably the true hero in my life story. If it had not been for his genuine concern and following through and tracking down the phone number I had dialed on the camp phone that day, our grandparents would have never known that we were still alive. Mr. Durham looked beyond our dirty, neglected appearance and saw two downhearted young teenage boys, with good manners.

So, how does my life story end? I'm not completely sure, but today my new life will began, because today I marry my best friend.

Made in the USA
Charleston, SC
26 July 2016